"A strong, terse, flowing story told by a young Indian fighting with Crazy Horse. It sings of the best in man as well as the worst."—*Commonweal*

"Dark Elk's adventures take on quickening life as the result of Benchley's abundant gifts for narrative and characterization."—*The New York Times*

"The well-written story abounds with warmth, humor, and details of Indian life."—ALA *The Booklist*

"Will appeal to young people who find themselves torn between old and new."—*School Library Journal*

ONLY EARTH AND SKY
LAST FOREVER

HarperTrophy

A Division of HarperCollins*Publishers*

ONLY EARTH AND SKY
LAST FOREVER

by Nathaniel Benchley

ONLY EARTH AND SKY LAST FOREVER

ISBN 0-06-440049-2 (pbk.)

For CHARLOTTE ZOLOTOW
with love

NOTE:

The main events in this work of fiction are true, and as historically accurate as the conflicting records allow. (Eyewitness versions of the same event often contradict one another, and are bewildering to anyone trying to find out the truth.) Taking the broad view of things, it all happened—and is, as a matter of fact, still happening in a modified way today.

As for the language, I have tried not to make too close an approximation of the way the Indians spoke, or how their language would sound if translated literally; the Tonto or "heap big paleface" type of dialogue is also not suited to this story. I have assumed that the Indians had colloquialisms among themselves, and shortcuts to expression, and toward this end I have made the people speak what sounds most natural to the modern ear. It is walking a tightrope, either way.

36 Via d'Arancia 1972   N.B.

ONLY EARTH AND SKY
LAST FOREVER

1

The nights were the worst. I would lie awake, rolled in my buffalo robe and looking at the stars, as I listened to the sounds of the others in their tepees, wondering if I would ever have a wife. I would think that the stars had some secret which, if I could unlock it, would give me the answer. I had known many girls, more or less in passing, but the only one I ever wanted was the one who came and left like a shadow, or the memory of a dream. She spoiled all the others for me.

I was born a southern Cheyenne, in Chief Black Kettle's clan, but I was adopted by the Oglala Sioux when I was twelve years old. My father had been killed fighting the Bluecoats in 1868, the year of the treaty that supposedly gave the Black Hills to the Indians for "as long as the sun shines and the grass grows," and my mother was killed later that year, when Long Hair Custer surprised our village on the Washita River, and killed half a hundred Cheyenne, old men, women, and children. I survived by pretending to be dead, hiding under my mother's body and covered with her blood, while Long Hair and his pony soldiers burned the village and destroyed everything in sight. In memory of that event, many of us referred to the white men as "Washitas," after that. We called Custer Long Hair, because he let his hair grow almost to his shoulders, or sometimes Yellow Hair, because it was the color of grass that has dried in the summer sun. We also sometimes called him Squaw Killer. There were many squaw killers among the pony soldiers, and often killing was the nicest thing they did to the women. One of them scalped my mother.

So, from the time I was twelve, I lived with the Oglala Sioux, first at the Red Cloud agency, and then, when that became unbearable, with Crazy Horse in rapidly dwindling freedom. But I remembered the words and habits of the Cheyennes, many of which were similar to those of the Sioux, and I had many friends among the followers of Chief Two Moon, whose fate became linked with that of the Sioux.

2

I first saw this girl when I was visiting a friend in a Cheyenne village. We had been hunting together, but the game was scarce, and in the whole day we bagged only three prairie chickens, which are so stupid you can walk up and knock them over with an untipped arrow. Some people prefer to behead them with a rawhide whip, but no matter how you do it they're not much of a challenge. My friend, Lone Wolf, gave them to his grandmother to clean and cook, and then he and I sat in front of his lodge and began to make fishhooks, hoping we might have better luck next day on the river. The fishhooks were made from the ribs of field mice, and the matter of tying them to the horsehair leader was a delicate one. We talked as we worked, telling stories we'd both heard before, while Lone Wolf's brother, who was about eleven and was called Fat Bug, scampered around and pestered us with questions. His name may have fit him when he was a baby, but it bore no relation to the way he looked now; he was lean and wiry, and as irritating as a greenhead fly.

Suddenly, I was aware of someone passing near us. I looked up, and saw this girl with a round, gentle face, and eyes that were as dark and as deep as a moonless night. She wore no paint and her hair was not braided, which meant she was unmarried, and although she didn't look at me she knew I was looking at her, and her face, while unchanging, glowed. For a moment I was tempted to drop my fishhook and run after her, but better sense prevailed and I returned my attention to my work as though nothing had happened. But Lone Wolf had seen my expression, and he laughed.

3

"She's not for you," he said.

"Who?" I replied, trying to look innocent.

"Lashuka, who just walked by."

"What do you mean, she's not for me? Who said I wanted her?"

"Your eyes."

"I was looking at my fishhook."

He laughed again. "Whatever you say."

We were quiet for a moment, then curiosity took over my tongue, and I said, "Why did you say she's not for me?"

"Running Deer is there ahead of you. He goes to her lodge every night."

I had heard of Running Deer, but knew him only slightly. He was two years older than I, and was already a member of one of the warrior societies with three coups to his credit. He was boastful and sure of himself, and I didn't like him. "That doesn't mean I can't go there too," I said. "Unless her father has already promised her."

"Her father was exiled for killing another Cheyenne," Lone Wolf said. "He still has almost the full four years to go. She and her grandmother moved here from their village. Her grandmother is mean as a hungry bear. Take my advice, and look somewhere else."

"Oh-ho!" I said. "So she can't be married for four years?"

"She can be married any time she wants."

"Then why hasn't she married Running Deer?"

He shrugged. "Who knows? Perhaps she doesn't like him." Then he looked at me, and smiled. "For someone who claims to have been looking at his fishhook, you're taking a lot of interest in other matters."

"I'm interested in everything," I replied. "The only way to learn is to take notice of what's about you."

"All right, but see her grandmother doesn't take notice of you. You'll be the worse for it if she does."

Naturally this warning did nothing to turn me away, and that evening I went to the tepee Lashuka and her grandmother had set up at the edge of the village circle. The skins stretched across the lodgepoles were old and thin, and through them I could see the glow of the fire inside. I pulled the flap aside carefully, not knowing what would happen. Through the smoke I saw Lashuka looking down at the fire, while her grandmother squatted next to it and stirred an earthen pot. The smell of boiling turnips mingled with the smoke inside the lodge, and I could see I'd picked the wrong time to make my call. Before I could replace the flap, Lashuka looked around and saw me, and her eyes widened in surprise. Then her expression softened, and she almost smiled. Her grandmother spotted me, and Lashuka's face went blank, as the old lady rose from the fire and came toward me. She looked like an old and stringy bear emerging from its winter sleep, and she pointed a clawlike finger at me and said, "Who are you?"

"My name is Dark Elk," I said.

"What do you want?"

I swallowed. "I would like to speak to your granddaughter."

She saw the blanket I carried, to put around Lashuka's and my heads so we could talk in privacy, and she said, "What gives you the right to stand under the blanket with her?"

By now my mouth was too dry to swallow, and I simply said, "I want to."

"How many ponies do you have?"

"One."

She spat into the fire, and turned from me. "Go away," she said.

"I could get more," I began. "It's just that . . ."

"What *akicita* do you belong to?"

"The warriors haven't chosen me yet. I live at . . ."

This time she turned her back completely. "Go away," she said.

"I haven't had a chance," I pleaded. "My family . . ."

"I said go away!"

I looked at Lashuka, and although her expression didn't change, her eyes seemed to be pleading with me to obey the old lady, so I simply said, "I hear you," and let the flap fall back. I turned away, and almost bumped into Running Deer, who had suddenly appeared out of the darkness. He wore a single feather, a symbol of his coups, crossways in his hair, and his medicine bag and pipe were at his belt. On his bow arm he carried a blanket. He looked at me for what seemed like a long time, then grunted.

"How," I said.

"Go back to the Coffee-Coolers," he replied, and lifted the flap and went inside. This was a deliberate insult, because it referred to the agency Indians, of whom my stepfather was one. They were known derisively as Loaf-About-the-Forts, or Coffee-Coolers, who depended for their living on handouts from the white men. And this was the reason I'd had so much trouble with Lashuka's grandmother: having spent most of my time at the agency with my adopted parents, I had not had the chance to do any of the various feats of bravery that help a youth make a name for himself. The *akicitas,* or warrior societies, chose their members from the young men who'd been outstanding in some way—either on a hunt, or on a horse-stealing raid, or in battle—and the life I'd been forced to lead made any of these things impossible. The agency Indians were content to sit about and do the white men's bidding, trying to grow crops in stony soil and waiting for the Government to give them food and clothing. The supplies were always late and usually spoiled and inadequate, but many Indians were tired of fighting losing battles against the Bluecoats, and preferred this way of life to being hounded to death. At least, they argued, it was food, whereas, on the prairie, with the buffalo rapidly vanishing, there was nothing to look forward to except starvation.

These thoughts chased themselves through my head, as I stood in the darkness and watched the glow of Lashuka's lodge, wondering how long her grandmother would let Running Deer stand under the blanket. With some girls, when a line of young men formed outside, the mother or grandmother was strict in the amount of time, sometimes snatching off the blanket in the middle of the young man's talk, but it was clear Lashuka's grandmother had no such scruples—at least where Running Deer was concerned. The stars wheeled through the sky and the coyotes barked in the hills, and I watched the fire in the tepee grow dim, and finally go out. Only then, when all was dark, did Running Deer emerge and close the flap behind him. I thought of following him and confronting him about the insult he'd given me, but then I thought I'd serve my cause a little better if I got to Lashuka alone, without her grandmother. I had a feeling she liked me, but I wanted to be a little more sure of myself before I made any plans. There are many ways of winning a girl, including just running away with her and setting up a lodge of your own, but it's best not to try such things unless you're sure she'll come with you.

So for the next few days I waited and watched, hoping I might find her alone, but her grandmother was as alert as a fox and followed her everywhere. Very few unmarried girls go about without either their mother or grandmother with them, and Lashuka's grandmother was doubly careful because she was aware of the way I looked at Lashuka every time they passed. Lashuka was aware, too, but she knew better than to look directly at me. She simply pretended I didn't exist, until finally I began to wonder if I was wasting my time. Lone Wolf assured me I was, and he tried to get me onto more important things, like hunting and making arrows. I went with him, but my mind was still lurking around Lashuka's lodge.

Then one evening, when the sun had gone behind the hills

and the sky was the color of fire, I saw her coming up from the river. She was alone, carrying two skins of water on her back, and I looked quickly about but could see no sign of her grandmother anywhere. I went to her, and said, "May I talk to you?"

"As I walk," she replied. "I can't stop."

"Where's your grandmother?"

"Sick. She has the white man's cough."

I wished I could feel sorry, but instead I felt a small glow of cheer. "Very sick?" I asked.

"Not so sick she doesn't know how long it takes to go to the river and back." Her voice was soft, and her dress smelled of sweet grass, and I began to feel slightly dizzy. I was afraid of saying the wrong thing, and as a result I could think of almost nothing to say, but we were nearing her lodge and I tried to hold her until I could compose myself.

"Must you walk so fast?" I said.

She nodded.

"May I see you again?"

Unbelievably, she nodded once more.

"When?"

There was a long silence, while we came closer and closer to her lodge. Then, in a very low voice, she said, "Tonight, after she's asleep."

"I'll be by the river," I said.

She nodded again, and I dropped back so her grandmother wouldn't hear my footsteps. I can walk as quietly as the next man, but I was convinced her grandmother had the ears of an owl, and could hear anything. Lashuka pulled back the flap, and went inside without looking back. I could hear the old lady cough, and complain about how long it had taken to bring the water, and I smiled to myself as I went to look for Lone Wolf.

Later that night, when the lodge fires were out and the village was dark and quiet, I went down to the river and waited. There was no moon, but the stars were so bright they made a glow on the water, and I could see almost as well as in daytime. There was an occasional snort from the ponies in the corral, and somewhere an owl called, and I listened carefully to see if it might have been a signal. But it wasn't repeated, and the ponies became quiet, so I relaxed a little. I thought how humiliating it would be to be caught by a raiding party of Crows, and I wished I'd thought to bring, at least, my bow with me, but I was afraid if I went back to get it I might miss Lashuka, so I stayed where I was. A coyote barked once, but there was no reply.

I heard her coming while she was still far away. She made no more noise than a mouse in the grass, but my ears were so tuned to every sound that I even knew she was barefoot. I stood up so she could see me, and then she was beside me and I smelled the sweet grass on her dress again, and after a silent greeting we both sat down.

"I can't stay long," she said. "She wakes herself up coughing."

One thing I noticed about Lashuka: it is the custom for Indian girls to be quiet, and speak only when spoken to, and while she conformed to this in public, she offered more than the usual yes-or-no answers when she was with me. The other girls I'd known had either been shy or stupid, because they'd never offered more than a short answer to a direct question—usually "no"—but Lashuka opened up more, and gave the impression she might even offer an opinion if asked. There were many things I wanted to talk to her about, but I reasoned I'd better get the most important one over with first.

"Do you like Running Deer?" I asked.

She looked at me with her large eyes, and smiled. "Why do you ask?"

"I want to know if I'm wasting my time."

"If you were wasting your time, would I have taken the chance of coming here alone?"

I thought about this a moment. "I guess not."

"What else would you like to know?"

Here she was making the questions and forcing me to give the answers, and I was embarrassed because it was a new position for me. "Lots of things," I replied. "It's hard to know where to begin."

"I suppose you'd like to know about my father."

"If you want to tell me."

"You know he killed another Cheyenne?"

"I was told that." I knew the penalty was automatic—four years' banishment, with whatever extra punishments the murderer's attitude deserved. A man could have his tepees burned, his ponies shot, his possessions destroyed, all depending on how he took the banishment, and on his reason for killing a man in the first place. Lashuka's father, she told me, had had a long series of misfortunes that led up to the final, fatal quarrel. In the first place, she was his only child, and he had therefore adopted a son to take his place in battle when he got too old to fight. (Usually, young men from sixteen to thirty-five did all the fighting, and a man stayed a warrior until his son was old enough to succeed him.) The youth her father adopted turned out to be lazy, slightly dishonest, and finally, as the hardest blow, he became a *winkte*, one of those men who dresses like a woman, does women's work, and even makes love like a woman. They are supposed to have good medicine, and a child named by a *winkte* is considered fortunate. But as a warrior a *winkte* is less than no good at all.

So her father had to continue fighting, even after his medicine weakened, and he was wounded more often than the younger and more agile warriors. Then a young man came courting, and promised her father fifty ponies for her hand (the palms of *my* hands became wet when I heard this). They smoked a pipe on the agreement, offering the pipe first to the earth, then to the sky, and then to the four great directions, and arrangements were made for the wedding. But then, when it came time for the young man to deliver the ponies, he brought only four, saying that the rest would be along shortly. Her father was suspicious but let the wedding proceed, saying it would be canceled if the other forty-six ponies were not delivered, and it then turned out that the young man had no such ponies and had no intention of delivering them. He tried to take Lashuka away by force, saying she was now his legal wife because the ceremony had been performed, and her father rushed into his lodge, came out with a hatchet, and threw it at the young man, cleaving his skull. Her father was banished that afternoon, and set up his tepee, as the law required, three miles from the village. Her mother stayed behind to care for him (she could take him food and visit in the daytime, but she could never spend the night), and Lashuka and her grandmother moved to the present village, where I met her.

When she was through there was silence, and we both stared at the starlight on the water. "Then you weren't really married," I said, at last.

"Not really," she replied.

"I mean, you didn't . . ." I couldn't think how to finish the sentence.

"No," she said. "I didn't."

"That's good."

There was another silence, and then she said, "What else would you like to know?"

I swallowed once, took a deep breath, and said, "Will you marry me?"

Very gently, she said, "Ask my grandmother."

I knew how much good that would do, so I said, "Will you just come away with me? Now?"

She shook her head. "That would be one more thing," she said. "My father couldn't stand it."

13

"But I'll get you ponies! I'll . . ."

"No," she cut in, more firmly.

"Then how do I ask your grandmother? She won't even speak to me!"

"You heard her. Until you have something to offer, she won't listen to you."

"Then I'll have to go off and . . ." I tried to think what I'd have to do to impress her grandmother, but I couldn't imagine any feats that would be daring enough.

"That's right," Lashuka said, after a few moments. "You'll have to go off and."

"Will you wait for me?"

"That will depend on how long it takes. I can't become an old woman, just waiting for you."

"It won't be long. I promise."

"Good."

That appeared to end the conversation, and she stood up.

"Can't you stay?" I asked.

She shook her head, and as I stood up she said, "Don't follow me," and walked quickly away. I followed at a distance, watching her until she disappeared into her tepee, and then I turned toward my bed. I saw a figure watching me in the darkness, and even without seeing his face I could tell it was Running Deer. He came closer, and said, "I told you to go back to the Coffee-Coolers." His voice was low, as though soothing a wild pony.

"I heard you," I replied. I wasn't going to start anything, but I wasn't going to retreat either. I stood where I was, waiting for him to make the first move. As he got closer, I could see he had his hatchet at his belt. He came just to within arm's reach, then stopped.

"If you're wise, you'll do as I suggested," he said.

"I may not be wise, but I don't obey insults."

He thought about this for a moment, fingering the hatchet at his belt. I kept my arms loose, ready to grapple if he should come at me. Finally, he said, "How does one insult a prairie chicken?"

He was trying to goad me into attacking him, but after what Lashuka had just told me I could afford to let him talk. "I don't know," I replied. "Why don't you try?"

He hesitated briefly, then said, "I have better things to do with my time," and turned away.

I watched him disappear into the darkness, and my small smile of triumph was dimmed by the fact that I had no idea how to impress Lashuka's grandmother. It would have been one thing if I'd been a member of an *akicita* and could go out on horse raids or war parties, but I was only a guest in the village. Somehow, and without waiting too long, I would have to achieve a feat of such bravery that I'd be recognized as a promising warrior, able to share in the spoils. But how? Certainly there was no chance at the Pine Ridge agency, so I'd have to do it out here. It's easy to say, "I will be brave," and it's something else again to prove it. It's not brave, for instance, to attack a bear with no weapons; that is simply stupid. A man can be brave in war or on a hunt, but where else? I decided my only answer was to go into the Black Hills,

15

purify myself, and ask for a vision from the Great Spirit *Wakantanka*. There are some things that are beyond the power of mortal man to decide, and this was one of them. If I deserved to have Lashuka at all, the Spirit would at least tell me how to go about it, and the rest would be up to me.

The Black Hills, so called because the pine forests on their slopes are so thick as to appear black, are the holy mountains where the Spirit and also the Thunderbird live, and no man who has seen the lightning flashing among the crags could doubt that this is the center of the world. The tears of the Spirit formed the lakes throughout the hills, and their purifying water is used to baptize children and to heal the sick. I remembered dimly when I, at the age of fifty moons, had been taken into the hills to be baptized, and I remembered the feeling of the cold, clear water on my brow, as my mother's mother and the medicine man pronounced my name. This would be the place where I would have my vision.

The next day, after telling Lone Wolf my plans, I mounted my pony and set off. As you approach them, the Black Hills look like an uneven ridge on the horizon, and often there are heavy clouds over them, with small tongues of lightning flicking about. Coming closer, you see that the hills are in some cases mountains, and everything towers above you and makes even the largest person feel small. The air around you speaks softly with the voices of wind, trees, and water, and when the Thunderbird beats his wings, the roar and the crashing drown out all other sounds. You are as meaningless as a leaf in a waterfall, and your loudest voice no greater than the squeaking of a mouse. I dismounted and led my

16

pony through the trees, hoping my instinct would take me to the right place.

There came a thinning of the forest, and I could hear the sound of water tumbling over stones. The air was suddenly cooler, as I emerged from the trees onto the shore of a small lake, into which water cascaded from the uphill side. It was so clear you could see the white stones on the bottom, and where the stream left the lake the grass was tall and lush. A great blue heron stood motionless on the far side, its curved neck and long beak poised above the water. A dragonfly darted back and forth, hunting smaller insects, and its wings made a shiny blur that glowed in pale colors. Here, clearly, was the place for me; I would spend the day and night fasting and purifying myself, and when the sun rose on the second morning I would make my prayer.

Then I heard another sound, above the plinking of the water; it was the sound of heavy footsteps, both animal and human, and with it was mixed the clank and clatter of metal. My first thought was that it was a pony soldier, who had somehow followed me without my knowing it, but my better sense told me no one had come my way; I knew I'd been alone since I left the village. The pony soldier didn't live who could catch me unawares. Then from the trees across the lake appeared a bearded, dirty, white man, leading a burro onto which was strapped a mound of odd equipment—the beast was loaded down with bags and tools and blankets, until it looked like a walking pile of baggage. The white man led it to the water for a drink, and then he saw me, and his eyes grew round and wide and he shouted. I couldn't hear what he said, but I understood well enough what he did; he reached into the baggage and pulled out a rifle, aimed it at me, and fired. The bullet chipped a tree beside me, and snarled off like an angry hornet. The man reloaded quickly—he had a repeater rifle—and this time kneeled to take aim, and I ducked into the trees just as another bullet whined past my head. I ran back into the woods, remounted my pony, then rode slowly down to lower ground, wondering what had happened to the world.

We who revered the *Paha Sapa*—our name for the Black Hills—knew that its earth contained a yellow metal, put there by the Spirit and to be used only in praise of his greatness. The white men, however, went slightly crazy when they found this metal, and the word that it was in the Black Hills brought hundreds of them flocking from the east like noisy crows. But the treaty of 1868 said clearly that the land was ours, and ours forever, and it never occurred to me that I might find a white man in one of our holy places—and be shot at by him, for no reason at all. Someone had to have an explanation, and the only person I could think of was Red Cloud, the chief of the Oglalas who had arranged the treaty in the first place. If he knew what this white man was doing, he could explain it to me, and if he didn't know, then it was time he found out.

I headed my pony out of the hills and southeastward toward the agency at Pine Ridge, where Red Cloud was living in fulfillment of his part of the bargain. The mere thought of the agency depressed me, but I knew of no other place to go.

2

Coming out of the Black Hills, you cross a stretch of badlands before reaching the White River, which you follow upstream to the Red Cloud agency. The badlands are named not for anything that happens there, but for what doesn't happen— they are bad for growing, bad for forage, and bad for hunting. They are stretches of rugged, rocky soil, and even the eagles wheeling in the sky have trouble finding food. As I rode over the dismal landscape, I thought of Lashuka's father, forced to live off by himself, hunt by himself, and lead the life of an outcast for four years, and I compared him with my adopted father, living in the comparative security of the agency. But I wondered if even the life of an exile might not be better, because at least he was his own master. He might be shunned by others, but his life was his own.

The soil is better along the White River, and the tall buttes on either side are footed in scrubby greenery. Off to the south rises the pine ridge that gives the area its name, and the trees are handy for all sorts of construction. The main drawback is that the land that can be used for farming is small in size, poor in quality, and hard to work, and has the extra hazard of droughts and grasshopper plagues. The white men said they would turn the Sioux into farmers within four years, but in all that time only one attempt was made at farming, and it was destroyed by the grasshoppers.

As I approached the agency I could see the hundreds of lodges and camps spread throughout the area, and then the pine-log buildings that made up the agency itself. There was the high wall of the stockade, and inside it a warehouse, a barn, several rooms and offices, and the two-story house belonging to the agent, a little man named Dr. J. J. Saville, who had been sent by the Episcopal Church in Denver as the man best able to take care of the Indians. What made them think that, no one will ever know. The Sioux called him "our white man," and treated him like a servant. Then there was a smaller stockade, belonging to a man named Deer who was the trader, and on the banks of the river a sawmill that worked by steam. A mile and a half away, across and up the river, was Fort Robinson, another stockade, where the Government had put several companies of Bluecoats, a move that angered many of the Indians and frightened just as many more. Wherever there were Bluecoats there was also trouble, and those who had come to the agency to get away from trouble were unhappy at the thought.

I went first to my family's lodge, because the very least I owed them was to tell them what I'd been doing. I found my adopted mother by the fire, staring glumly into a skillet in which she was trying to fry a lumpy mass of something. She looked up at me, and her face brightened for a moment; then she returned her attention to her cooking. She seemed much older than when I'd last seen her, although no more than two moons had elapsed. After I had rubbed and tethered my pony and given him water I looked into the skillet, and asked what it was. She hesitated a moment, then said, "Bread."

I looked closer. "What kind?"

"It's the only thing we can do with the food they give us," she said. "The thing they call pork is so bad even the dogs won't eat it, and all you can do with the bacon is heat it to bring out the grease. Then, if you mix the grease with some of their flour and fry it, you have bread." As an afterthought, she added, "Of a sort."

"What about meat?" I asked. "Don't you get beef anymore?"

"Every five days we all go to the stockade, and they let

some cattle loose. But they're all eaten up quickly, and we go back to this." She shook the skillet, to keep the bread from sticking.

"And that's all you have?" I asked. I remembered the food as bad, but not like this.

She shrugged. "Now that you're back I might boil a dog for you, but that's only because it's a special occasion."

"Don't do it for my sake," I said. I looked at the dogs that were sniffing around the fire, and didn't see one that even faintly appealed to me. For my taste, a dog must be young and fat to be worth cooking, and all these were old and stringy. Even cooked with herbs and turnips and wild onions, they'd have tasted of nothing but fur and bones. "Where's Father?" I asked.

She hesitated a moment before saying, "Up at the stockade, I guess."

"Does he have business there?"

"I don't know."

"Then why would he be there?"

"You'll have to ask him."

It was clear she either didn't know or didn't want to talk about it, so I changed the subject and told her what had happened to me in the *Paha Sapa*. "I'm going to tell Red Cloud about it," I said. "I think he ought to know what's happening."

"He knows."

"What's he doing about it?"

"I don't ask about these things. They're no concern of women."

22

"It was Red Cloud who made that treaty, so he should protest when they break it." I knew there was no use discussing it with her, but I couldn't believe Red Cloud wouldn't be concerned. "I'm going to see him anyway," I said. "If he isn't doing anything about it, I'd like to know why." She said nothing, and I left her staring into the skillet and gently shaking the formless lump of bread.

It was October, the Moon of Changing Seasons, and as I approached the stockade I could feel the first tinge of autumn in the air. There was something else in the air, too, and it had nothing to do with the season; there was a mood of anger and discontent, like the humming of many swarms of bees, that seeped through the camps and the lodges and the groups of people. You couldn't see it, but you could feel it and almost taste it, and it was all the more ominous because not a single thing was happening. There was just this mood, ugly and resentful, and you had the impression that people were waiting for something, anything, that would touch off the explosion. It made my skin crawl, and I walked faster.

In the six years since the treaty was signed, Red Cloud had grown visibly older, and more weary. His large nose and mouth were bracketed with heavy lines, there was a slight curl to his upper lip, and his eyes had a heavy-lidded look of sorrow. He wore a fringed buckskin shirt and trousers, and his long hair was unadorned except for a single eagle feather at the back of his head. The white men's Government had given him a house, but it was squalid and dark and the roof leaked, and he stayed out of it as much as he could. He was sitting in front when I approached him, and I remember

23

thinking how odd his Indian clothes looked in the white man's setting. I thought if he was going to live in a house he should wear white man's clothes, but of course I didn't say this; I simply felt pity at what he had once been, and what he was now. I told him what had happened to me, and his expression hardened slightly, but he didn't seem surprised.

"He came by the Thieves' Road," he said, quietly. "There are many like him."

"What road is that?" I asked.

"It was cut by Long Hair, some moons back. He and his soldiers cut a road for the men who dig the yellow metal."

"He can't do that! It's against the treaty!"

"I have complained to the Great Father. He tells me he will keep them out."

"But he hasn't! A *Washita* just shot at me!"

"Have patience. There are other things more important."

"I don't know what!" In my anger I forgot myself, and I could see I'd angered him.

"The matter of food," he said, in an even voice. His eyelids lowered slightly and he went on. "Until the people here can eat properly and be properly clothed, I cannot worry about white men in the *Paha Sapa*. I have done what I can, and the Great Father Grant has said he will do the rest. Please let me be the one to decide."

"I'm sorry," I said.

"It is good to be young and impatient," said Red Cloud, "but it is also good to be old and experienced. There must always be the balance."

24

There was nothing more I could say, so I excused myself and left him. Only as I walked away did the real force of my rudeness come to me. Red Cloud had been the one who stopped the white men's invasion of our country in 1867; he had led the Sioux and Cheyennes in a series of attacks that wiped out the first detachment and kept any more from coming in; and he had refused to give up an inch of land until the whites agreed that all the territory of the North Platte, through the Black Hills to the Bighorn Mountains, should be ours forever. For me to tell him what to do about the whites was not only rude, but arrogant, and he would have been right to give me a much harder rebuke than he did.

As I left the stockade there was a commotion near the gate, and I heard hoarse shouts and saw a group of men standing in a circle around two others who were fighting. The shouts were animal-like and unintelligible, and it was hard to know if the shouter was being killed or was doing the killing; whatever it was, they had the high-pitched tone of fury that comes with deadly combat. Two white men looked on with faint amusement, and as I passed I heard one say, "Somebody oughta do that red nigger a favor and shoot him." I knew enough of their language to understand, and to resent the contempt in the voice. A terrible feeling came over me; I can't explain it, but I sensed I had to break up the fight, and as I pushed through the circle of watchers I saw that the man doing the shouting was my adopted father. He was red-eyed and incoherent, and he had his opponent down and was trying to beat out his brains on the ground, while his opponent had

25

his teeth sunk into one wrist and with his hands was twisting my father's genitals. I leaped onto my father's back, put a wrestling hold under his arms and behind his neck, and lifted him clear. He struggled for a moment, and then the whisky, which had brought on his rage, took full control, and he collapsed in my arms. I let him down on the ground, then helped his battered opponent to rise. He also was drunk, and he stared at me as though trying to see me through clouds of smoke.

"Who you?" he asked.

I told him.

"Want to fight?" He tottered, and almost fell.

"No, thank you." I looked at the spectators, who were enjoying the whole thing. "Who gave them the fire cup?" I asked. Nobody spoke, and I repeated the question.

"Deer," said one man, referring to the trader. Then, as though reading my thoughts, he added, "Save your breath. Deer hears only the sound of money."

I looked down at my father, whose face was covered with dust-caked spittle and whose wrist was torn and bleeding, and I wondered where he'd got the money to buy whisky. He looked small and tattered, and bore no resemblance to the proud warrior who'd adopted me six years before. I leaned down, and gently picked him up and put him across my shoulders, and carried him back to our lodge.

I approached the lodge from downwind, and before I reached it I could tell that my mother had put a dog in the kettle to celebrate my return. The smell of boiling dog is unmistakable, although it can vary with whatever herbs and spices are added, and while it's considered a delicacy of sorts it cannot compare, even at its best, with roasted elk, or buffalo. And, as I said before, none of these dogs was what you would call a tender morsel. But, since she'd done it with the best intention, I had to pretend to be pleased. Things were bad enough as it was, without my giving needless offense. Her expression didn't change as I took my father into the lodge and laid him on his buffalo robe, and I took it this was a usual happening. I covered him, then went outside and looked in the pot.

"You shouldn't have done that for me," I said, trying to sound pleased. "You should have saved it until you needed it."

"One time is as good as another," she replied. "And it isn't every day that you come home."

The thought of calling this dismal camp home depressed me, and to change the subject I said, "Where does he get the money to buy whisky?"

"I don't know," she said, as she pulled a steaming piece of dog from the pot and examined it. She dropped it back, and added, "I think Lame Moose steals it."

"Is Lame Moose the one he was fighting with?"

She nodded. "Every time Lame Moose finds white men's money—he always says he just found it—he buys whisky, then he and your father drink it all, and fight. They're very good friends."

"This is new with him," I said. "What makes him do it?"

She shrugged. "What else is there to do? He feels he's lucky to have a friend like Lame Moose, who'll share it with him."

"Is that the only friend he's got?"

"He used to be friendly with Duck-Who-Walks-in-a-Circle, but they had a fight. A real fight."

"About what?"

"I didn't ask. But he bit off the end of Duck-Who-Walks-in-a-Circle's nose, and that was the end of their friendship."

I thought of my plan to do great deeds to impress Lashuka's grandmother, and it became clearer than ever that this agency was not the place to do them. Whatever I did, it would have to be someplace else. But that wasn't anything I wanted to mention now; homecoming is no time to announce a new departure. I sniffed the pot and smiled as though in pleasure, and was rewarded by the look on my mother's face. It didn't take much to make her happy, and every bit of cheer was that much gained. I remembered the ominous feeling I'd had on the way to the stockade, and it came to me that right here might be the happiest place in the whole agency.

The next day something happened that made a strong impression on me, so strong as to guide the course of my future actions. In a way, you could say it was an answer from the Spirit to my unasked question about what kind of deeds to do, because it showed me the one thing that was worth striving for. The fact that it was impossible wasn't clear until much later, but that didn't make the trying any less worthwhile.

As often happens with big events it started off in confusion, and only little by little did the facts come out. The first thing I knew that something was happening was when I heard the sound of pounding hooves, and war whoops. My father was deathly ill from his bout with the fire cup, and I was sitting beside him, trying to get him to take a bowl of dog broth for strength.

"Why do I need strength?" he asked, turning his head away. "It would be better just to lie here, and die with dignity."

"Don't say that," I told him, holding out the horn spoon. "That is as bad as to surrender in battle." I'd never been in a battle, but I knew all the rules.

"This battle was lost long ago," my father said. "It was lost when the white men first came to the shores of our country. There are too many of them, and those who try to fight them are foolish."

"Don't *say* that!" I repeated, angrily. "You've always told me how if you're pure and strong and brave you'll win out in the end, so how can we lose? The white men are evil, so they must be the ones who'll lose!"

He almost smiled, but his face was too shrunken to make the gesture. "I did tell you that, didn't I?" he said. "Well, keep on believing it, then. Who knows? But for me . . ." He didn't finish the sentence, because at that point there came the thunder of hooves and the shouts, and I put down the bowl and ran outside.

From all quarters mounted Sioux were riding toward the

river, some with rifles, some with pistols, and some with bows and arrows or lances, and they were shooting in the air and generally making as much noise as they could. I leaped on my pony and joined in the charge, caught up in the excitement but not having any idea what it was about. I rode up alongside one northern Lakota—the Sioux refer to themselves as Lakotas, or "The Men"—whose face was painted and who carried a lance festooned with scalps, and I called to him and asked what was happening.

"Bluecoats!" he shouted, pointing with his lance. "Look ahead!"

I looked, and there, through the dust and smoke, I could barely see a column of pony soldiers coming down the valley from Fort Robinson. There weren't many—it was a very short column, and they were moving slowly—and from all sides the Lakotas were converging on them, and circling around. If it was going to be a battle it would be a short one, because there were several hundred Indians, and I hoped I'd get there in time. I wished I were armed with something better than my hunting knife, but I'd come off in such a hurry I hadn't thought to bring my bow, and then it occurred to me that if I could count at least one coup I'd have made a start toward my reputation. (I should explain that counting coup, or striking an enemy without trying to kill him, is a much braver act than shooting him, and a man with many coups is one to be admired.) My heart leaped at the thought of the action, and I lashed my pony's sides and gave a high-pitched, warbling cry.

When I reached the crowd of mounted warriors who were circling the troops, I realized that nobody was shooting *at* anybody; all the shots were fired in the air, and the soldiers hadn't even unslung their guns. The warriors were just riding around them, closer and closer, and trying to frighten them into firing the first shot in anger. Then, of course, the real killing could begin. But the soldiers didn't take the bait; they rode quietly along, staring straight ahead, and I saw one or two of them running their tongues across their lips. There were twenty-seven of them, including the officer who rode at the head, and they were reining their horses tightly to keep them from bolting. Every now and then one of our warriors would ride in close and try to jostle a soldier's horse out of line, but except for a slight jump or a sideways skitter they all held their formation. I decided to try—after all, it would be a coup of a sort—so I selected one soldier and charged right at him, howling like a wolf.

I closed in on him and could see he was pale, even for a white man, and his eyes grew big and round as he saw me come at him. My knee brushed against his, and I could smell the disgusting smell of white men's sweat, and I made a grab for the wide-brimmed hat that was perched on his forehead, but he ducked his head and I missed. Then I was away, back with the circling warriors, feeling the heady rush of joy that comes with danger. I remembered small things about the trooper, like how his eyelashes seemed almost white as he stared at me, and that the hair that grew down the side of his face was yellow and kinky. He didn't look old—perhaps about my age—and it surprised me to think the Bluecoats would have young men in their ranks. It had always seemed, from the way they behaved, that their men were old and hardened criminals, but this trooper just looked young and very frightened. I decided on my next charge to go at him again, and see if I could make him bolt.

I never got to make another charge. Things happened so fast it was hard to tell what was going on, but suddenly there were other Lakotas among us, riding straight at the troopers, and when they reached the column they turned and faced the rest of us, and *began to beat at us* with their pony whips and war clubs! There were a great number of them, and they formed a ring around the soldiers, forcing us back and clubbing those who tried to break through. They were led by Young-Man-Afraid-of-His-Horse, the head warrior of the Oglalas, and by young Sitting Bull, the nephew of Little Wound, and they were all agency warriors, big and tough and mean. Two of them knocked young Conquering Bear, a Brulé, from his horse and put a bow across his neck and stood on the ends until his face turned black. The sight of Sioux fighting Sioux was so terrible that I fell away from the action, not wanting to have any part in it.

In this way the agency warriors escorted the troopers all the way to the stockade, and led them inside. Before the gates closed behind them I saw splintered bits of wood lying on the ground, and I remembered yesterday having seen a long tree trunk, which workmen had been trimming down to make a flagpole. It was now in many pieces, showing signs of furious hacking.

32

But the action wasn't over yet. As soon as the gates closed, a number of warriors began gathering bales of hay and putting them against the walls, intending to set fire to the stockade. The crowd was in such a frenzy it would have done anything to show its outrage, and short of a fight with the troopers a fire seemed the next best answer. I still didn't know what had caused the uproar, but it seemed to be an explosion of all the anger I'd felt in the air yesterday. Before anyone could actually start a fire, the Oglalas came out of the stockade and forced us all back, and then Old-Man-Afraid-of-His-Horse and Red Dog came out and began to talk to us, asking for calm and reason.

It was only then that I found out what had been going on. It seemed that Dr. Saville, the agent, had thought it would be a good idea to have a flagpole, but to many of the northern Lakotas a flagpole meant soldiers, and they wanted nothing about the soldiers on their agency. They protested, but Dr. Saville didn't take them seriously, so this morning a number of them got painted up for battle and went in and hacked the pole to pieces. Dr. Saville lost his head and sent to Fort Robinson for help, and that was what started the whole riot.

When you look at it calmly the flagpole itself wasn't so important, but it was a symbol of what was going on; and the Lakotas' anger, which had been building ever since the word of Long Hair's going into the *Paha Sapa*, needed only this small thing to make it explode. Red Cloud himself, the chief of all Lakotas at the agency, had not realized how deep was the anger at what Long Hair had done. When I saw him he'd been more concerned about food and clothing than anything else, and even now, after what could have grown into a full-scale war, he didn't even come out to talk to us. He let others do the talking for him, while his warriors held us off.

And that was what decided me. When things had reached the point where Sioux were fighting Sioux, when our holiest places were being defiled as casually as a dog lifts his leg, and when proud men were reduced to drunken beggars who squabbled among themselves, then the time had come to get at the root of the trouble, and rip it out. That root, of course, was the white man—the *Washita* who could do nothing that didn't bring on grief—and the best thing I could do would be to join those who still opposed him. Go with what were called the hostiles, and if we couldn't drive the white men out we could at least go down fighting, and know our fight had been in a good cause. When you come to think about it, it was the only cause, because every other pathway led to ruin. I felt that Lashuka would be proud of me for my decision. I made it as much for her as for myself, because I couldn't think of my own future without thinking of her as a part of it.

Next day, I told my family I was going off to hunt. My mother never questioned me about such things because I was old enough to make up my own mind, but I could see she was disappointed.

"You only just got here," she said, which was as close as she would come to a rebuke.

34

"I know," I replied. "But think how good it would be if I could come back with some buffalo meat, or antelope, or elk. Wouldn't you like that?"

"Where are you going to find that kind of meat?" my father asked.

"There's still game, if you look for it," I replied. I didn't want to tell him that I was really going to be hunting white men, but I think he guessed it. I know he did, because his next remark was made looking toward the stockade.

"Be careful the game doesn't shoot back at you," he said. "Its weapons reach a long way."

"I'll be careful," I said, breezily, and left them looking after me. I headed my pony north, toward the camp of Crazy Horse, the one Oglala whose name was still feared by Crow and Pawnee and white man alike.

3

Crazy Horse was away when I reached his camp. He was leading a party of warriors against the miners in the *Paha Sapa*, but Black Shawl, his wife, made me welcome and gave me food. She was quiet, and thin, and her eyes seemed always to be looking at something over the horizon. I learned from others that her infant daughter—hers and Crazy Horse's only child—had died a few moons before of the white man's coughing sickness, and she now worried every time he went out on a raid. His grief had made him wild, and he took chances that no sane warrior would take, but his medicine was strong and he was never hurt. Even his warriors were concerned at the chances he took, and his enemies were terrified. A captured Crow said it was a known fact that Crazy Horse could never be struck by a bullet and that his own gun hit whatever it looked at, but his wife wasn't quite so sure. She went about her business of drying meat, making clothes, tanning hides, and cooking for those who came to see her husband, but she counted the days until he returned. Her eyes kept wandering to the direction in which he'd left, in the hope of seeing him the moment he came into view. He was almost thirty-three, which is getting old for a warrior, and she couldn't escape the feeling that his medicine must some day lose its power.

To put my time to best use until he returned, I decided to go hunting. With no family lodge to sleep in, I needed one of my own, but the covering for a single tepee took about fifteen buffalo skins, and I didn't have even one. I reasoned that, if by some wild piece of luck I could get even two buffalo, I would then have something to trade with, and start gathering possessions. All Lakotas share with those in need, but a man's pride demands that he not be a burden.

I went to Black Shawl and, trying to sound as though I were an expert hunter, said, "I think we could use some fresh meat. Would you like buffalo, or elk?"

She looked at me to see if I was joking. "Whatever you bring back will be good," she said, quietly.

"I think I'll go for buffalo," I said. "I may be gone a few days."

"Do you have food?"

It hadn't occurred to me that I might need food other than what I shot, and while I was trying to think of an answer that wouldn't sound too stupid she went into her lodge and came out with a parfleche of dried meat and a bag of *wasna*, which is a mash of ground berries, corn, and meal that warriors eat on a raid, to prevent making the smell of a fire. "You may not need it," she said, as she gave it to me, "but it never hurts to be prepared."

I thanked her, and set off in the direction of the Powder River. Only a few years ago this whole country was black with buffalo and alive with antelope and elk, and while you can still find them every now and then, the herds are scattered and much thinner than before. The white men and their iron road were what first drove the buffalo away, and then the hunters came and followed the buffalo and killed them by the hundreds and thousands. They took the hides, or sometimes just the tongues as counters, and left the carcasses to rot in the sun. Our living was their sport, and if you look at it one way they might as well have been killing us as the buffalo.

I rode for two days without seeing anything more than snakes and jackrabbits and prairie chickens. I was beginning to wonder if there was something about me that drove the game away—if I had some bad medicine that needed to be cleansed—and while I was thinking this I looked up at the sky and saw an eagle, wheeling overhead. I watched him closely, because you can tell a lot from the way an eagle behaves, and I saw him glide high above the crest of a hill, then double back, reversing his course of flight. That meant there were men on the other side of the hill. I got off my pony, unslung my bow, and walked forward carefully. My heart beat faster at the thought they might be white men, and that I might begin my career by rubbing out one or two of them. White men's scalps are thought worthless as trophies, but when you have no deeds at all to your credit they are better than nothing.

As I neared the crest of the hill I tethered my pony, then crept forward until I was just below the ridge. Then, working on my stomach, I built a small pile of stones, and when it was higher than my head I raised up and looked around the side of it into the valley below. For a while I could see nothing, and then I realized that right in front of my face, not an arm's length away, an arrow had dropped into a clump of sagebrush. I drew it out, seeing that the three wavy lines on the shaft marked it a Cheyenne arrow, and the set of the iron head showed it was for hunting. (The head of a hunting arrow is set in the same line as the bowstring notch; a war arrowhead goes across the notch line so the head will fly flat, and slip more easily through a man's ribs.) So there was a Cheyenne hunting party somewhere below, and with nothing to fear I stood up, went back for my pony, and rode over the ridge to find them. I took the arrow along, to return to its owner.

There was a wolf call from the valley; I answered it, and then it came again and I saw my friend Lone Wolf come out into the open. We greeted one another with pleasure, and he told me he was with a hunting party from Two Moon's village, over on the Powder River. I told him my story, and when I was through I hesitated and then, as casually as I could, said, "Is that girl—uh . . . Lashuka—how is she?"

He laughed. "The same," he said.

"And Running Deer?"

"A strange thing about Running Deer," Lone Wolf replied. "He started off with us on this hunt, and on the second morning he woke up with a terrible pain in his jaw. He told us that, since his medicine is the jaw of a deer, the pain was a warning he'd bring bad luck to the hunt, and he'd better go back. Nobody could argue, so he left."

"What gave him the pain in the jaw?"

"Only he knows that. All I know is it didn't look bad to me."

I thought about this, and could imagine him going back to be alone with Lashuka, and my teeth grated. Then I remembered the Cheyenne arrow I'd found. I brought it from my quiver, and said, "Is this yours?"

He glanced at it, and nodded. As he took it he looked embarrassed and said, "I shot it at an eagle."

"That's no way to catch an eagle," I told him.

"I know. But it was the only thing I'd seen all morning."

An idea began to form in my mind, and I said, "Will you help me build an eagle trap?"

"We're out here to get food. What do you want with an eagle?"

What I wanted was some eagle feathers, which he could take back to Lashuka as a present from me, but I couldn't quite bring myself to say it. Better get the eagle first, and then make it look like an afterthought. So I said, "Black Shawl asked me to get one."

He looked at me hard. "That's a sacred business," he said. "You don't catch an eagle the way you would a toad."

"I know." In my desire to get something for Lashuka I thought I could probably avoid the more sacred parts of the eagle hunt, and just build the trap. I'd seen it done, when I was much younger, but I'd never tried it myself. "We don't have to make a sacred rite of this," I said. "Just get one eagle, that's all."

Lone Wolf didn't like the idea. "That's not the way it's done," he said. "Besides, I'm here for more important game."

"All right," I said. "I'll do it myself."

He was upset. "It isn't just the trap. You've got to build a purifying lodge, you've got to . . ."

"I said we wouldn't make this a sacred rite," I cut in. "I'm just going to dig the pit."

He thought a few moments, then said, "I can't tell the others I've been wasting my time on an eagle trap, when they're . . ."

"Don't bother yourself about it. I told you, I'll do it myself."

He was about to say something more, when from nearby

41

came the two, clear notes of a quail call, and we both sank to the ground. It is a known fact that the call of the quail brings instant exhaustion to anyone who hears it, and the only thing you can do is lie down and wait for your strength to return.

"Well, there goes your hunting," I said, at last. "You'll never shoot anything big today."

Lone Wolf was too depressed to speak. Finally he said, "Do you still plan to dig your trap?"

"As soon as I'm able. If I can get it done today, I'll get in it before dawn tomorrow. If you *want* to help me, you can tell your friends the truth—that you heard the call of the quail, and were through hunting for the day."

"I'm not sure I have the strength to dig a hole," Lone Wolf said. "That was awfully close."

As though in answer to his words the bird called again, from what seemed like the grass at our feet. Lone Wolf's eyes rolled upward, and his tongue sagged out. "Kill it, can't you?" he groaned.

"I can't see it!" I reached to where I'd dropped my bow. "If I could see it, I'd throw something at it."

"Maybe if we shout it'll scare it off," he suggested, so we both shouted and made wolf calls as loud as we could. There was a whirring of wings and the quail rose from the grass, skimmed away like a low-shot arrow, and vanished. Lone Wolf took a deep breath. "We should have thought of that sooner," he said. "That second one just about finished me."

42

If I hadn't been so intent on getting something for La-shuka I'd have realized I was defying almost every sort of omen and taboo known to man. I was planning to perform a sacred rite without purifying myself; I was planning to catch a sacred bird for an unsacred purpose; and I was determined to do this in spite of two clear warnings from the call of the quail. If ever the Great Spirit had tried to warn someone it was just now, yet, as soon as I had the strength to stand I began to look around for a place to dig the trap. Lone Wolf pulled himself up and followed me, with a face of deep gloom.

We found a spot on a ridge, away from the trees, and we marked out a patch about six feet long and two feet wide. Then, with our knives, we lifted squares of sod away and put them to one side, after which we dug the pit down about three feet. We put the loose earth in our blankets and carried it off a short distance, where we piled it around in a way to look like gopher holes. Then we cut sticks and laid them across the pit, and on top of them put the pieces of sod we'd first taken off, and finished the covering with bits of grass and whatever was lying about. We left a hole just big enough for me to get into. Then, on our way back to Lone Wolf's hunting camp, we shot a jackrabbit, cut it into pieces, and put them in my sack.

When the hunters heard I came from Crazy Horse's camp they assumed I was an Oglala, and were cordial. They admired Crazy Horse, and although they, as Cheyennes, considered themselves the world's fiercest warriors (the Crows maintained they were simply insane) they were still respectful of Crazy Horse's reputation. They called themselves *Tsis tsis tas* which means "The People," or "Human Beings," and the Sioux called them *Shahiela*, or "Red Speech," meaning they spoke a foreign tongue, but as I've said, many people spoke both languages, and they had many of the same customs.

Back in the old days, when the Lakotas had only dogs to pull their travois, it was the Cheyennes who first gave them ponies, the Cheyennes having got them by devious means from the white men. The first white men to invade the country, who came from the south, brought horses, and they changed the Indians' way of life. The white men may have brought disaster to the land, but you can't forget they also brought the horse. Although a lot of people would gladly go back to using dogs, if it would get rid of the whites.

At any rate, the hunters asked me about Crazy Horse and what he was doing, and I had to admit I didn't know much more than what Black Shawl told me. When they heard I'd come from the Red Cloud agency they asked me about that, because there were many different stories about what life down there was like, and on that subject I was able to tell them a good deal more. The agency people were singing of all the great gifts you would get if you came down there to live—the food and the clothing and the guns and ammunition—and many people had believed them. I told the hunters how bad the food and clothing were, and also how Dr. Saville had some stupid notion that all the Indians should be counted. He claimed the Great Father needed to know how many there were so as to be able to feed and clothe them all, but anyone in his right mind knows that to be counted is the worst possible luck in the world, and of course the Indians refused. This made for a lot of bad feeling, in addition to what was there already. I told the hunters about the flagpole incident, and they agreed that to go back to the agency was to do nothing less than ask for trouble.

One of them, a lean and scarred warrior named Flat Nose, said to me, "We saw signs of buffalo to the north today. We're going to try to catch them tomorrow. Would you like to join us?"

Normally I would have leaped at such an invitation, but I had this eagle trap so firmly in mind I could think of nothing else. "Well . . ." I replied, "when do you start?"

"Before light."

"I'd like to very much, but I have this . . . trap to care for. I must be there before light, and I don't know how long after. If I don't, the game may escape." He nodded, and that was the end of it. Looking at it now, I can see I was being offered one more chance to give the whole thing up, but when a person is blinded by love he doesn't see the foolish things he's doing. What it meant, of course, was that I'd have to get along without Lone Wolf's help, but at the moment that didn't seem too important. He'd helped me dig the pit, which was the hardest part of the job . . . I thought.

45

So in the middle of the night, when the stars were still bright and the moon had just gone down, I got up and made ready to return to my trap. The others were stirring, and there was the feeling of quiet excitement that comes at the beginning of what may be an important day. It's hard to describe, because everything is the way it usually is, but lurking in the darkness is the possibility of great things to come, and it gets into your bones.

"All right," Lone Wolf said, quietly. "Good luck."

"You, too," I replied. "If you shoot too many, save one for me." This was a joke, because every man keeps his kill in a buffalo hunt, and only the old and the sick have meat given to them, which is shot by special hunters. Lone Wolf laughed.

"Yes, Grandmother," he said. "I'll save the choicest bits for you."

"The hides are what I need the most."

"You can still come with us, you know."

"No, thank you. The eagle is more important."

He must have sensed that nobody could be as stubborn and as stupid as I was without a reason, and that reason could only be a woman, because he said, "If we come back this way, I'll stop by and see how you fared."

"Good. I'll be glad to see you." In my mind, I saw myself giving him a handful of eagle feathers to take to Lashuka, and I added, "I might even ask you a favor." With that, I mounted my pony and left.

When I got near the trap I led my pony into the woods

and tethered him where he couldn't be seen from above. Then, working only by the light of the stars, I moved the last bits of sod and grass near the hole, took the pieces of jackrabbit out of my sack and put them on top of the covering, and then climbed into the hole. Lying on my back, I pulled the sod in place over my head, getting my eyes and mouth full of dirt as I did, and finally, when I had the whole thing covered as best I could, I lay back and waited. This was where Lone Wolf would have been the most help, to cover the pit from above and make it look completely natural, but that was just something that couldn't be helped. I reasoned that if an eagle was hungry enough, the bait would draw him down.

I lay on my back, silently praying for the strength I was going to need, and I slowly became aware of the coming of day. Little chinks of gray showed through the covering over my head, then the gray turned to blue, and the blue to bright white. I could see small patches of sky, which was a help, and I only hoped that any eagle up there wouldn't be able to see me as well. Time passed, and as the sun began to warm the ground I could smell the jackrabbit, even through the turf and grass. I wondered if it would attract a coyote or a wolf, and figured I'd have to take care of that situation if and when it happened.

I waited. And I waited. And I waited. The air inside the pit grew hot, and the back of my neck itched with sweat and fallen dirt, and though I strained my eyes through the small holes I could see nothing in the sky, and hear nothing coming near. Once, I thought I heard my pony snort, and wondered if something had alarmed him, but he didn't snort again and nothing came near my pit. I was lying in a darkened hole and the world was somewhere else, and I began to wonder if I might be dreaming, or having a vision. Many men had visions that affected the entire course of their lives, and I thought that if this was my vision, then my future didn't look too bright. I might as well be on my burial scaffold, wrapped in the mourning blanket, with the birds tearing at my flesh. I could almost hear the beating of their wings in the air, and then the silence as they landed, and the slow *pick-pick* of their talons on the ground as they came close.

Something tugged at the covering above me, and tugged again, and I realized it was tearing at the bait! Then I saw the eagle's head, and its great yellow eye, and the feathered shoulder of a monstrous wing. I took a deep breath, gauged where the feet would be, and thrust my arms upward and clutched, then jerked down. There was an explosion of screaming and beating from above; the covering shattered and showered me with dirt and twigs and grass, and as I pulled the eagle toward me it tore my forearms with its beak and sank its talons into one wrist. Fire shot through my arms but I held on, trying to get one hand loose to grasp the eagle by the throat—the method was to wring its neck—but I couldn't get the proper hold, and the wings beat my head like clubs until I almost lost my senses. It was the beak that finally made me lose my grip; the beak started slashing at my face, and as I brought one arm up to cover my eyes the eagle wrenched free, and was gone. I lay there for I don't know how long, one arm still covering my eyes, and a hot shame burning through my body that was worse than the burning of the wounds.

When, at last, I pulled myself out of the pit, the sun was sinking behind the hills. My hands and arms and chest were covered with dried and dirty blood, my hair was full of twigs, and clinging to my belly, stuck there by a glob of eagle dropping, was one tufty feather from its underside. I plucked it loose and hurled it from me, and it settled softly to the ground. So much for a present for Lashuka.

Wearily I found my pony, untethered it, and led it down to a stream where it could drink and I could bathe. The cold water helped a little, and when I had cleaned and dried myself I ate a little *wasna* from the bag. I was bleakly wondering what to do next, when very softly from behind me came a wolf call. I turned and saw Lone Wolf, standing near the ridge. Then he came down, and for a moment neither of us said anything.

"How was the hunt?" I asked, at last.

He shrugged. "They went into Crow country. We didn't have enough to follow." He looked at my arms, but didn't comment.

"You were right about the eagle," I said. "It needs more preparation than I gave it."

He nodded, but still didn't say anything, and I was grateful to him.

"Next time, I'll do it differently," I said.

Lone Wolf looked at the sky. "Flat Nose said something that depressed me," he said.

"What?" I asked, wondering who could be more depressed than I.

"He said this was about the end of the buffalo. They're going to get fewer and fewer, until there are none left."

"I suppose that's right. Unless we can keep the whites from killing them all."

"That's just it—we can't. And without the buffalo, we'll all starve or freeze to death."

"So what does Flat Nose want to do about it?"

"He's thinking of going in to the agency. I wonder if maybe he isn't right."

"He's wrong!" I said, suddenly angry. "He's wrong, wrong, wrong! I've lived on the agency, and I know what it's like—rotten food the dogs won't eat, shredded blankets, and no-good clothes, and firewater that makes men crazy! I'd sooner be dead than live there again!"

"You don't mean that," said Lone Wolf.

"I do!"

"Well, I don't know. You're alive, and someone's in charge of looking after you. Out here you have to hunt for your food, which gets scarcer and scarcer, and if you do anything wrong the Bluecoats come after you. I don't know if it wouldn't be better to go back, and let someone else do the worrying for a change."

"Listen to me," I said. "Flat Nose may feel that way because he's old and aching, and tired of fighting. But you and I are young. We've just begun to live like men, and we *can't* give up! We've *got* to live the way we are supposed to, and fight anyone who tries to beat us down! What is there to live for, if you just fold up like an old tepee?"

"There's always a reason to live. The first thing is to recognize what you can do, and what you can't."

"You're never beaten if you don't admit it. If enough of us get together, we can chase the whites out of here like so many antelope."

"Don't I wish that were true. That's not what Flat Nose thinks."

"Forget Flat Nose! Think for yourself!"

"And you think we can beat the whites out of here?"

"I think we can try. And if we all work together, we can rub them out to the last man."

"You talk pretty warlike."

"I'll be just as warlike as they. If they leave me alone I'll leave them alone, but the minute they try to take my land, or turn me into a Coffee-Cooler, then watch out." I was aware I was talking very big and very loud, but it angered me to see Lone Wolf feeling defeated. An older man I could understand, but not someone my own age.

"I don't know," Lone Wolf said. "There seem to be a great many problems, and very few answers." He took a deep breath, spat out the piece of grass he'd been chewing, and said, "Will you stay with us tonight?"

I thought a moment, then said, "No. I want to be in

camp when Crazy Horse returns." There wasn't all that much hurry, but I didn't want the other hunters to see the signs of my disgrace. Also, I didn't want to get into an argument with Flat Nose.

"Then I'd better go," said Lone Wolf.

"Good luck."

"You, too." He cleared his throat. "Is there anything I should tell Lashuka?"

"Yes." I tried to find the words, and finally said, "Just tell her to have patience."

"I hear you," Lone Wolf said, and turned and went away.

4

Crazy Horse was known to the Oglalas as "Our Strange Man." All through his boyhood he was called Curly, and his skin and hair were so light that some mistook him for a captive white. But his father, also named Crazy Horse, was an Oglala holy man, and his mother was a Burned Thigh, or Brulé, Lakota, sister of Chief Spotted Tail. Curly had been trained in hunting and warfare by the great Minneconjou-

Oglala warrior High Back Bone, known as Hump for short, and although Crazy Horse was good in everything he did, he was never boastful. He preferred to stay quietly in the background while the others sang of their deeds; he had had a vision that one day he would be leader of all his people, and he saw no need to boast. It was also part of his vision that he would never be harmed, except by one of his own.

When I first saw him, he was riding into camp at the head of his warriors. He was dressed, as always, like the man in his vision: white buckskin shirt and blue leggings, one feather in his hair, and his braids, which came to below his waist, wrapped in beaver fur. A small, red-backed hawk was on his head, and although I couldn't see it, a brown medicine stone was tied behind one ear. This was his costume, and for war he loosened his hair and painted a white streak of lightning on his cheek. The column of warriors was quiet; there was none of the rejoicing that comes with the return of a successful war party, and it developed that although they had managed to harass some miners and burn a few outbuildings, the white men seemed to be everywhere, and trying to rub them out was like attacking a swarm of gnats. You might get a few, but the end result was unchanged. All they really had to show for the venture were some pack mules of white men's goods, which would be useful for the coming winter.

When I told Crazy Horse why I wanted to join him, he looked at me for what seemed like a long time before he answered. I saw the scar on his face, right beside his nose, where a man named No Water had shot him in a rage about a woman, and this reminded me of Running Deer, whom I would gladly have shot. I saw myself shooting Running Deer—no, better, besting him in hand-to-hand combat, wrestling him to the ground and putting my foot on his neck, while Lashuka made a trilling noise of encouragement for me—and while I was dreaming this way, Crazy Horse said, "You are sure you know what you are doing?"

"I am sure," I replied.

"How many ponies do you have?"

I swallowed. "One."

"You'll need more than that. You can't ride all day on the same pony you take into battle."

"I know. I haven't had the chance to get more."

He gave me three of his ponies, and let me stay in one of his lodges until I could make one of my own. Most families have more than one lodge because you need one for storing provisions, one for cooking in bad weather, and as many more for sleeping as the size of the family requires. Crazy Horse's family was small, and he had enough extra room to take me in. So I became, in a sense, his adopted son, although at eighteen I was too old for adoption. Still, my life at the agency had held me back in many respects, and there was a lot I had to learn. My bout with the eagle was proof of that.

Later a messenger arrived, saying things at the Red Cloud agency had turned very bad. It seemed that Dr. Saville was so set on having the Indians counted that he said there would be no more food or clothing until they agreed. This made for much discussion and arguing among the Indians, with Red

Cloud himself saying they should not allow it, but others defied him and moved in and let themselves be counted. There was much bad feeling, and many felt that Red Cloud had lost his medicine if he could be so easily defied. And then the winter struck, and things were worse than ever. No food came through, and people had to eat their scrawny horses. All things considered, it was much worse for those "friendlies" at the agency than it was for those of us "hostiles" who had to fend for ourselves.

The snow was deep that winter. There was very little visiting between the camps, and people were kept up to date by news walkers, who plodded through the snow, either on horseback or on snowshoes, passing along whatever information they had. For the most part, people stayed in their lodges, the men making arrows and other weapons, and the women doing their usual household chores. If the weather permitted, the children would go out and play on their buffalo-rib sleds, and a few hunters would search for stray elk or buffalo, but the chances were so thin that nobody went very far afield. For someone like myself, who was burning to do great deeds, the winter seemed without end.

But finally the spring thaw came, and with it the need to get more horses. Many horses had died that winter and so, as soon as those remaining had had a chance to fatten up on the new grass, a raiding party was organized against the Crows. I didn't have to volunteer; Crazy Horse knew of my impatience, and was afraid only that I might do something foolish. He, who frightened his own warriors with his deeds, was still aware of the difference between bravery and stupidity, and he didn't want me to run needless risks just to make a good showing. His old warrior-teacher, Hump, had been killed on a raid that should never have been made, and he didn't want that sort of thing to happen again.

"Above everything else," he told me, "never shoot blindly. Shoot only when you're sure of hitting, and close enough so you can't miss. And remember—a moving target is hardest to hit, so keep moving yourself. Always press forward, and you'll find the other man will fall back. Never put your weapon down, and try never to shoot your last arrow or bullet; you may need it more another time. Those are just the basic rules; the rest you'll have to learn for yourself."

I nodded, fearful only that I might not do well enough to please him.

A crier went around the camp, calling all who wanted to go on the raid to come to Crazy Horse's lodge. He went four times, as was the custom, and soon the various warriors began to arrive. In all there were about twenty, and after Crazy Horse had explained the mission they began to dance and sing, each one taking a song that showed his feelings on the matter. Some would mention a girl's name, and say he was going to do brave deeds for her, and the word would get around and the girl would come and listen, which made it impossible for him to change his mind later on. One song, for instance, was sung by a warrior named Gone Goose, and it went:

> For you, Yellow Flower, I will take the Crows' ponies;
> For you I will bring them all home.

I will smite those who follow
And try to destroy us;
My arrows will slip through their ribs
Just for you.

He sang this several times, and Yellow Flower, who came when she heard her name, seemed to think it was a good thing all around. How many horses he later brought back, I wouldn't know.

It was here that I learned a strange thing, which was that some warriors are afraid when they go into battle. I, who had never done it, was excited by the idea, but the more I listened to the songs the more I realized that some of the older ones had to convince themselves that everything was going to be all right. One song said: "I am afraid of the old man's teeth, I will go either way," which meant that a man is going to die anyway, so it's better to die in battle than get old and toothless and be a burden to the tribe. An odd way to buck up your courage, but I suppose it worked.

The women had a great deal to do with this keeping up of courage, too, because they were sure to torment the life out of any man who turned fainthearted. One song in particular pointed this up by saying: "If you are afraid when you charge, turn back; the Desert Women will eat you." In other words, after the women get through with you you'll wish you had died in battle. Then there was one sung by the onlookers, who weren't going out on the raid, and they sang: "My friends, only stones stay on earth forever; use your best ability"—this, you understand, is a very rough translation.

I never felt that song cheered anyone very much, being sung as it was by those who were going to stay at home, but I later heard charging warriors shout, "Only the earth and the sky last forever!" which of course is one way of looking at it, when you're facing the enemy. Others would call out "Today is a good day to die!" Another approach to the same problem.

At any rate, the dancing and the singing went on, with more and more people gathering to watch, and the beat and the excitement began to mount. Someone brought out a drum, which helped with the rhythm, and the beating of the drum and the pounding of the feet made my whole body throb. The singing went around the circle, and at one point there was a silence and I saw that people were looking at me, so I stepped forward and closed my eyes and made up a song about how I was going to do great deeds for Lashuka and make her see she needed to be my wife. I really didn't feel I had to convince her as much as I did her grandmother, but I felt it would sound strange to be singing a war song about impressing someone's grandmother, so I used Lashuka's name instead. It was my first war song, and I didn't want to clutter it up with unnecessary facts. It went:

When I think of ponies, Lashuka, I think of you.
When I think of great deeds, Lashuka, I think also of you.
I think of you both day and night, and everything I do, I do for you.
I will do such great deeds they will astound you;
And you will live in my lodge forevermore.

As I say, it was my first war song, and composed in a hurry. Of course in Sioux it rhymed, and the first line didn't make

59

it sound, as it does in English, that Lashuka resembled a pony. In Sioux it was rather tender, I thought, but that's what happens when you translate something into another tongue. What's tender in one tongue can sound fairly flat in another. At any rate, my heart was in it.

The dancing kept up all night, and as the sky began to turn pink we circled the village four times and then started out. The women had made our provisions ready, and they sang strong-heart songs and made the trilling noise that gives men courage, and I must say that in spite of not having any sleep I felt as though I could accomplish anything. I was a little stunned, but my blood was still pumping to the rhythm of the drum, and in my mind I was unbeatable. This will show you what a war dance does.

Twenty warriors is a lot for a simple horse raid, but we might be going deep into Crow country and Crazy Horse didn't want us to be caught badly outnumbered. He sent two men far out in advance as scouts, and two more wide on our flanks, and then assigned two others, myself included, to ride in the rear with our extra horses. The idea of being a horse guard didn't appeal to me in the least, but I knew better than to question him. I just hoped he was saving me for more important work later on.

It is one thing to be all keyed up for battle and then start fighting, and it is something else to ride all day at a slow walk, herding a lot of skittish horses. By the middle of the afternoon my eyes felt like lead and my mouth tasted of iron, and my temper had worn down to the point where I was shouting at the horses and offering them all sorts of injury. I didn't beat them, but I told them several things I'd like to do to them, and once, when I was telling a certain horse what the buzzards would do to his liver when I was through with him, I looked around and saw Crazy Horse riding beside me.

"Do you hate horses?" he asked, quietly.

I took a deep breath, realized I'd been childish, and said, "No."

"That is a strange way for a man to talk, unless he hates," said Crazy Horse.

"I'm sorry," I said.

"Don't apologize to me. Tell the horse."

I waited, and he kept looking at me, so feeling like a fool I said to the horse, "I'm sorry."

After another pause he said, "The horse forgives you. This time." And he rode off.

Late in the afternoon, we made camp. The scouts came in, and others were sent out on guard duty, and since nobody had seen any sign of the Crows, we felt it safe to make a fire. I was staring into it in a stunned way as I chewed on a piece of dried meat, when I realized that Crazy Horse was squatting beside me. He said nothing, so I said nothing, and for a while we both looked at the fire. Finally he spoke.

"Do you know the most important thing to learn?" he asked.

"What?" I could think of several important things, but they could only be learned through experience.

"Patience," said Crazy Horse.

I thought he was talking about the afternoon, and I said, "I'm sorry about that. I wasn't thinking."

"I don't mean patience with horses. I mean patience with everything. I have seen many good ambushes spoiled, just because the young men didn't have the patience to wait."

I had nothing to offer, so I was quiet.

"Even in battle you need patience," Crazy Horse went on. "You need patience to wait for the right shot, you need patience not to expose yourself needlessly, and you need patience to wait for the right time to get away. You might have to hide all day some time, in order to escape." Here was talking the man who frightened his own warriors with his daring, and he was counseling me on patience. I tried to understand why he was doing this, but the reason didn't become clear until later.

We rode on for two days and then, when the clouds in the west were beginning to glow, one of the forward scouts came galloping in. His expression showed nothing, and his voice was calm; he might have been reporting a dead coyote.

"Crow village," he said. "Next valley, beyond the ridge."

"How big?" Crazy Horse asked.

"Big," replied the scout. "And a big corral, with many ponies."

"Guards?"

"I saw no guards. This is so deep in their country they must think they don't need any." His eyes showed a glint of pleasure; otherwise his face remained blank. A scout is never supposed to show excitement.

"They'll have guards at the corral tonight," Crazy Horse said. "Nobody is so secure he doesn't put out some kind of watch."

I was about to volunteer to go ahead and look for guards, when I remembered that you don't ask to be a scout; it's an honor to be chosen, and you have to wait for it. I saw Crazy Horse looking at me, and for one wild moment I thought he might be considering me, but then his eyes traveled on, and he chose two other warriors to go ahead. That was only sensible, because I'd never done this kind of thing before.

We rode slowly forward until it became dark, then we stopped. Crazy Horse selected a spot near some trees, where the ponies could be concealed, and when they were all tethered we ate some *wasna* in the darkness, not daring to make a light. I was so excited that my tongue was dry, and the *wasna* stuck in my mouth, and only by swallowing hard was I able to get it down. We were gathered in a circle, and I heard Crazy Horse say, "Now. Bear Brains, you take men with you to get ponies from the corral. Black Fox will bring three men with me to get those tethered in the village. Dark Elk,"—My throat closed as he mentioned my name—"you and Laughing Hawk will stay here, and guard our ponies until we return."

In spite of myself, I said, "*What?*" and there was a short and ugly silence before Crazy Horse continued.

"Your first job," he said, as though I hadn't spoken, "is to make sure no Crow comes near. You must rub him out before he can spread the alarm. Your next job is to be ready, when you hear us coming back, to get our ponies moving, because we will want to travel fast." The way he talked made it sound important, but in my black disappointment I could think of it as nothing but woman's work, and I didn't trust myself to speak. I knew now why he'd given me the talk on patience.

When he had finished, those who were going with him painted themselves and made their final adjustments, then slipped away into the night, leaving Laughing Hawk and me staring after them. Laughing Hawk was younger than I, but had had more experience. He seemed more resigned to being left behind.

"The easiest part of the raid is getting the ponies," he said, looking up at the sky.

"What else is there?" I asked.

"Getting home again." He sniffed the air. "There are many who never make it."

"What do you smell?"

"I don't know. I think it may snow."

"This time of year?"

"It has happened."

I looked at the sky, and could see a thin layer of clouds creeping across the stars. The air was cold, but no colder than usual at night. It was the Moon of the New Grass, which the white men call April. "Well, it can't snow hard enough to hurt us," I said.

"Perhaps, but we'll leave tracks for the Crows to follow."

"They won't if they know what's good for them." I was

beginning to feel brave again, instead of humiliated.

Laughing Hawk shrugged. "Ever since Hump was killed, Crazy Horse has taken many men with him on a raid. He wants no more needless deaths. But when you're this deep in enemy country . . ." He shrugged again, and dug his fingers into his *wasna* pouch.

It came to me that Laughing Hawk liked to talk as though everything was dangerous, to make himself feel better for having been left behind. He was really as disappointed as I, but was trying not to show it. This made me feel better, and I decided to boast a little. "Have you counted many coups?"

He looked at me in the darkness, and after a moment said, "A few. And you?"

"Only one. On a white pony soldier."

I could tell from his silence he was impressed, and then he said, "You mean in battle?"

"Almost." I told him the story of the flagpole incident, making it sound as dangerous as I could.

"I heard about that," Laughing Hawk said, when I was through. "I heard the Bad Face would take no part in it."

He was referring to Red Cloud, using the tribal name in a scornful way. It was a sign of how Red Cloud's medicine had left him that people should speak this way, and remembering my talk with him I felt I should come to his defense. "It's not all his fault," I said. "He has to think about . . ."

Before I could finish the sentence, one of our ponies whinnied, then another, and there was a sudden flurry of stamping hooves. Laughing Hawk and I raced to where the ponies were tethered, and in the darkness could see a mounted man among them. He was flapping a blanket, trying to make them stampede, but they were well enough tied so all they could do was snort and kick. I shouted, and Laughing Hawk grabbed his rifle and fumbled with a bullet, but before he could get it loaded the man took off into the night, and we could hear the hoofbeats slowly getting fainter. Then there was silence.

"You frightened him off," Laughing Hawk said, with disgust. "If you'd kept quiet, I could have shot him."

There wasn't much I could say, because he was right. I'd shouted out of instinct, and it had been the wrong thing to do. "Well, at least he didn't get the ponies," I said, lamely.

"No, but he'll spread the alarm. The whole village will be waiting for Crazy Horse when he gets there."

I tried to think of a cheerful reply, but there was none. Whatever happened to the raiding party would be my fault, and mine alone, and it was not a pleasant feeling.

We calmed the ponies, and made sure there was no one else about, and then we sat down to wait. By now the stars were gone and the wind had picked up slightly, and it had an edge to it like a knife. I began to believe Laughing Hawk's idea that it might snow, because the air had that smell about it that comes before a storm. A coyote yapped and howled in the hills, and was answered by another, and we both listened to hear if they were real coyotes or men signaling. A real coyote has a howl that makes it seem much nearer than it really is, and while a man can imitate the yapping and the general idea of the howl, he can't give it that quality that fills the air from far away. Laughing Hawk and I concluded that these were real coyotes, although to be safe I got up and made a quiet tour of the area. It was hard to see anything, but I was as sure as I could be that we were alone.

I don't know how long we waited; it seemed like all night. But the sky was still black as a bear when Laughing Hawk said, "Listen!" and put his ear to the ground. I did the same, and felt, as faint as a falling feather, a distant tremor that was the pounding of many hooves. Laughing Hawk stood up. "Let's get ready," he said. "I think they're coming fast."

We loosened the ponies' bindings, and took the thongs off the legs of those that had been hobbled, and by the time we were through we could hear the rumble of the approaching herd. Crazy Horse must have cleaned out the entire Crow corral, because the sound was like the booming of the Thunderbird in the *Paha Sapa*. Our ponies became nervous and skittish, and we had all we could do to keep them from bolting. Then out of the night came Crazy Horse and his warriors, mounted on Crow ponies and herding what seemed like several hundred others. In fact it was nowhere near that many, but the darkness was full of snorting, blowing horses, and it was hard to count. One of the warriors shouted at us to join them, so we mounted and brought our own ponies into the galloping throng. The men were laughing and shouting, partly out of pleasure and partly to keep the herd going.

Gradually the pace slowed, and by the time the sky began

to lighten we were down to a walk. Crazy Horse had wanted to get as far as he could while it was still night, and now that daylight had come he felt he could afford to slow down. The ponies needed the rest, and so did the men. They had been able to silence the Crow guards, and make off with almost half the herd without waking the village. They hadn't been able to get the best horses, which were tethered among the lodges and too well-protected, but this didn't make much difference. I was riding alongside Bear Brains, and I asked if they'd seen anything of a single Crow scout before they reached the village. He looked at me with interest, and his deep-set eyes seemed to take on the green of his face paint.

"Why?" he said.

"We saw one," I replied. "He got away before we could catch him." I saw no need to add that he almost got away with our ponies as well.

Bear Brains told me they'd heard the scout coming, and Black Fox shot him off his horse with a single arrow. He asked how close we'd been to him and I said, "Not very," wishing I'd never brought the matter up.

"It was a good thing," he said. "If Black Fox had missed, we'd have had bad trouble."

I remembered what Laughing Hawk had said about getting home from a raid, and I said, "Do you think they'll follow us?"

"They'll try," said Bear Brains, and that was all. He passed his hand across his eyes as though to wipe away fatigue, then settled into silence. I noticed that his paint was slightly smeared.

There was no sun that morning; the sky changed from black to gray to lighter gray and then to white, as the snow came down hard. We rode on, huddled in our blankets and hoping the snow would cover up our tracks, but it never got deep enough for that; it blew, and drifted, and stung our faces, and far from covering our tracks it made them plainer, because it caked in the ponies' hooves and then came off any time we crossed a rocky area. Someone following could almost have counted how many we were.

The Crows caught up with us late in the afternoon. Crazy Horse had been looking back, almost as though wondering what was keeping them, and when he finally saw them in the far distance he stopped and glanced at the sky. The snow had let up, and there were still about two hours of daylight left, and I could see he was wondering if we could keep ahead of the Crows until nightfall. It was possible, but the men and the animals were tired, and the added strain of pushing hard for two hours would weaken our ability to fight when we finally had to. He split us into two groups, one to keep the herd moving at a steady pace and the other to form a line of battle in the rear, facing the oncoming Crows. For some reason I couldn't believe that a battle was near; it seemed all sort of quiet and natural, like something that happens every day.

When the Crows got close, I saw why Crazy Horse was so feared. With a loud shout of "Hoka hey!" he charged straight at them and then, instead of shooting from his pony he dismounted, snapped off a shot, and mounted again, leaving one Crow warrior kicking on the ground. He made every shot count, and he rode at the Crows so hard that they scattered in front of him, firing blindly. I was so intent on watching him that I missed two Crows who got around the side of the herd, and they came in at me, firing and shouting and scattering the ponies. I had only my bow and arrows, and I shot at one of them and missed, hitting his pony in the rump, and while it didn't do any great damage it took that Crow out of the fight for a while, because his pony let out a scream and bolted. The last I saw of him he was trying to work the arrow loose, and at the same time keep some sort of control.

One thing I learned that afternoon, and that is when you're in a fight you only know what's happening where you are; you have no idea how the rest of the battle is going. I remember mostly Crow warriors circling and ponies plunging, and I remember shooting until all my arrows were gone but not being sure of hitting anything squarely. I remember the noise, the shooting, the shouts, and the screams, and then I remember seeing a gun lying in the snowy, churned-up ground, and getting off my pony to pick it up. The next thing I remember I was lying flat on my face in the mud, while Crazy Horse stood over me and fought off the three Crows who'd been trying for my scalp. The back of my head felt as though it had split open, and there was blood on my shirt, and I realized that one of those Crows must have hit me with a war club when I leaned over for the gun. I pulled myself to my knees just as Crazy Horse crushed the skull of one of the Crows, and then the other two decided they'd had enough and fell back, giving me time to rise. I was still attached to my pony by the tether rope that I'd looped in my belt, and I remounted, clutching the gun that almost cost me my scalp.

The Crows had managed to cut some of the ponies out of the herd, and with darkness coming on they seemed to feel this was the best they could hope for. They pulled away, taking their dead with them and staying well clear of Crazy Horse, who continued to charge at anyone who came near. Finally, when he saw the fight was over, he turned back, and his eyes had the look of a man coming out of a dream.

Black Fox had been killed, and several others including Laughing Hawk and myself wounded, but only one man was hurt badly enough to need a travois. This was an older warrior named Hangs-From-the-Trees, and he had been shot twice in the chest. You could hear the air hissing and bubbling as he breathed, and he told us not to bother with him; that his time had come, and he would rather die where he was than slow down the rest of us. But Crazy Horse wouldn't listen to him, and he had poles cut and lashed to a horse, then saw to it that Hangs-From-the-Trees was made as comfortable as possible in the hammock slung between the poles. Then we started off, in case the Crows should change their minds and come back at us during the night.

I remember very little about the rest of the trip home. My head made a roaring noise most of the time, and I saw mounted warriors with eyes that glowed like coals, and they were riding in the air and circling like vultures. Sometimes the glowing coals changed to wolf fangs, and wings would grow from their heads, and then they would look like men again, but be laughing like loons. It was very tiring, and there seemed to be no difference between day and night, but then things cleared a little, and I saw Black Fox's wife slashing her arms in mourning, and I knew we must be home. I groped my way to the tepee I had left what seemed like years ago, and as I sank onto my buffalo robe I remembered my vow to do great deeds. Some other time, I told myself. Right now, all I want is to sleep.

5

When I woke up, the lodge smelled of burning sweet grass. I opened my eyes slowly, trying to remember where I was, and the first thing I saw through the smoke was a figure that looked like a bear. It was making noises like a bear, too—growling and muttering and snorting—and I closed my eyes again, thinking I was either still having visions or I was about to be eaten. Either way it didn't seem to matter, because I didn't have the strength to do anything about it. I heard the noises come closer, and in spite of myself I opened my eyes again, to see what was happening. Then I saw that this thing had the head of a bear but the body of a man, and as it got still closer I recognized it as Low Bush, the medicine man. He crawled toward me, blowing sweet-grass smoke as he came, and rattling a medicine bag of bear claws, and I just lay there to see what would happen next. When the bear head was almost touching my face he gave a loud roar, then reached out and turned my head and roared at the back of it. It was then I realized he'd made a bag of some sort of medicine and tied it to the wound on my skull, and that was the first time I remembered being wounded. Slowly things began to come back to me, and I was aware that the pain was gone and my strength was coming back. Low Bush backed away, still growling, then watched me from the other side of the fire as he put on more sweet grass. I brought myself into a sitting position, wondering if I should say anything, but before I had a chance, Low Bush backed out of the lodge, and I could hear him talking to someone outside. Then the flap parted, and there was a flash of daylight that hurt my eyes, and Crazy Horse came in.

"How do you feel?" he asked.

"Better," I said. "Did I sleep long?"

"Two days."

I brought myself to my feet, and found that my knees were as loose as a bead necklace. "I just need to walk," I said, and fell down.

"You need to rest some more," said Crazy Horse, and with that he pulled back the flap and left. I lay there, remembering how, in spite of all my brave intentions, I had failed to do anything except get in trouble, and I vowed that, as soon as I could walk, I would set out to improve myself. So far, all I had done was prove that Lashuka's grandmother had been right in her contempt. I only hoped that none of it would rub off on Lashuka, while I was away and unable to defend myself. If the old lady wanted to, she could probably fill Lashuka's ears with all sorts of poison, and this is an unsettling thought to live with when you're so weak you can't even walk. I resolved to get well as fast as I possibly could.

There are many things a warrior must do that take practice. One is the matter of sliding down the neck of a running pony, clinging with one foot to his backbone, and firing a gun through his mane. This is hard even when the pony is standing still, and when he's running it's that much harder. When my strength returned, I decided that was one of the first things I'd work on, because I hadn't needed it at the agency and it was clear I was going to need it now. As an example, if I'd been able to ride that way during the raid, I could have picked up the gun without dismounting, and would never have been wounded. It was one thing for Crazy Horse to dismount during battle, and quite another thing for me. So, hoping I wouldn't look too foolish, I took my best pony and my gun, and set off to practice. I didn't have any bullets, but for this kind of thing I didn't need any.

75

The first three times, I fell off. Once you're started over a pony's shoulder it's hard to stop, and the first time I tried it the ground rushed up and hit me before I knew what had happened. But I gradually learned the trick of sliding slowly, and holding his mane, and clutching his backbone with the moccasin on one foot. Next came aiming the gun, and then doing the whole thing at faster and faster speeds. It was a slow business, and I lost a lot of skin off my shoulder and ribs from the falls I took, but I finally could do it. With no bullets I didn't know how good my aim was, but you can't waste bullets on practice, anyway. They're hard enough to come by, so everyone has to have an important target.

Then one day the word arrived that Red Cloud was going to Washington. It was said he was going to ask the Great Father for a new agent, claiming that Dr. Saville had been cheating on the rations, but Crazy Horse knew better. He knew that, no matter what the reason for the trip, every time an Indian went to Washington the result was more white men in the Indians' country, digging up the earth for the yellow metal. He was angry at the Bad Face for playing into the hands of the whites, and he decided to go down to the agency and try to stop the trip. A party of us went with him, hoping for some action. I now had seven bullets for my gun, having got them in a trade, and I wanted to see how good my aim was.

Laughing Hawk and I rode together, and he told me some of the things I hadn't known about the return from the horse raid. He asked me if I remembered singing, and I said no; all I remembered were the warriors with eyes like coal who swooped around and sometimes grew wings on their heads.

He laughed. "You sang almost the whole time. Wild, crazy songs."

"What were they about?" I wondered if I might have been singing about Lashuka.

"It was hard to tell. Hangs-From-the-Trees was on the travois singing his death song, and he thought you were singing your death song, too, so that made him sing his all the louder. The two of you just about drove the rest of us crazy. All we could do was grit our teeth and hang on, and try not to listen. Hangs-From-the-Trees finally died, but you kept right on singing."

I was embarrassed. "I'm sorry," I said.

"We understood. But we decided if you ever got to have a warrior name, we'd suggest it be Singing Elk. You really made the canyons ring."

The way he said *if* I ever got a warrior name was not very cheerful, but I knew he didn't mean it as an insult. It was all too clear I was a long way from being a warrior.

When we reached the bluffs surrounding the agency, we saw we were too late. A column of wagons was leaving, headed for the iron road that led to Washington, and we could do nothing but stand there and watch. Crazy Horse hadn't thought of making a fight; he had hoped he could reason with Red Cloud and try to persuade him not to go, but now he saw it was useless. His face was hard as he looked

77

down on the scene, and it seemed to me he was looking into the future, and seeing all the bad things that were still to come. His face was hard but his eyes were sad, and I felt the same sort of sadness. It was as though I had caught it from him, the way you catch the white man's cough, or spotted fever. He said something in a low voice, and He Dog, who was next to him, turned in question, as though he hadn't heard.

"My father once told me," Crazy Horse said, more loudly, "that one does not go to a hilltop for water, or to a white man for the truth. I wonder what lies they will come back with this time."

As I looked down at the clusters of lodges surrounding the agency I thought of my adopted parents, and wondered how they had managed during the winter. With Crazy Horse's consent I rode down from the bluffs and picked my way through the scattered campsites to where our lodge had been. There was a smell that hung in the air, which I cannot describe other than to say it was the smell of despair. Last year, at the time of the flagpole trouble, the air had been full of anger and resentment, but now it was nothing but bleak, hopeless despair. People moved slowly or not at all, and I noticed that there were almost no dogs or horses about; they'd eaten them all during the winter. Their clothes were rags and their blankets were in tatters, and I almost felt ashamed of myself for being well-clothed and mounted on a healthy pony. When I got to where our lodge had been I found only a flimsy *wickiup*, or lean-to, with an old man sitting on the ground in front. His face was deeply lined and his eyes were almost closed with sickness, and when I asked him about my parents I thought at first he hadn't heard me. I was about to repeat the question when, without looking at me, he said, "Maybe they went to the fort."

"Why would they do that?" I asked.

There was a silence, and then he said, "Some people thought it would help, if the soldier chief saw how poorly they were. They moved close by, to show him how they lived."

He didn't offer any more, and after looking around for a while I headed toward the fort. Here and there were skeletons of horses, the bones picked clean and white, but nowhere did I see a fire, or any sign of cooking. It was as though the whole encampment were slowly dying, the people having given up even trying to stay alive. I asked a few people about my parents, but nobody seemed to know anything, until one man said, "Was he the one who used to fight with Lame Moose all the time?"

"Yes," I replied, afraid of what was coming next.

"Dead," the man told me. "He and Lame Moose fell in the snow one night, and next morning they were dead. Frozen stiff as tree trunks."

"And my mother?" I asked.

"No one knows. She took him off for burial, and no one's seen her since. That was in the Moon-of-the-Dark-Red-Calf, and the snow was deep."

"Did anyone try to find her?"

He looked at me blankly, and I realized I'd asked a foolish question. People were too concerned with their own trouble to go off searching for someone in the snow. I thanked the old man, and turned away. The Moon-of-the-Dark-Red-Calf, which the white men call February, had been a long time ago, and if she hadn't been seen since, then it was certain she was dead. And probably better off at that. I remembered, dimly, how she had looked when I first came into their life: she'd had a round, pleasant face, with smooth skin and shining black eyes, and her eyes would seem to laugh every time she looked at her husband. He was lean and hard-muscled, and had high cheekbones and a massive nose that gave him a ferocious look when he was in war paint, but an oddly gentle one when scrubbed clean. They had been, in my eyes at least, an extremely handsome couple, and to remember what they had come down to made me almost sick. As I rode back into the hills I felt a mixture of relief, that their troubles should be over, and anger, at those who had caused the troubles. My heart was bad against the white men, and growing worse with every day that passed.

When I rejoined Crazy Horse and the others and told them what I'd heard, Crazy Horse simply grunted. He wasn't unsympathetic, but he wasn't surprised either.

"It's as well you left the agency last year when you did," Laughing Hawk observed. "If you hadn't, you'd probably have wound up the way they did."

"I don't know," I replied. "I keep thinking if I'd stayed around, I might have been able to help them."

"That kind of thinking does no good," said Crazy Horse. "If you try to relive the past it just makes you sad, and changes nothing."

While this should have been a cheering thought it did nothing to make my heart any better. As I saw it, there was no point fighting Crows and Pawnees and Snakes over such a simple thing as horses; the only real enemy was the white man, and all our energy should go to fighting him.

And I got a chance to do that just two days later. Crazy Horse had led us toward the *Paha Sapa,* where we could see the roads the whites had cut into the sacred hills, and late in the afternoon we saw a wagon train, winding its way below us like a lazy snake. The canvas wagon tops glowed like flowers with the sun behind them, and a quick look at the sky told Crazy Horse we didn't have time for an attack that day.

"We'll wait," he said. "Then, when they stop for the night, we'll go ahead."

We pulled back out of sight, leaving one man to scout, and as the sun sank behind the mountains and the valley turned blue with shadow, he signaled that the wagon train had stopped, and was forming its night encampment. In the gathering darkness, Crazy Horse led us to a spot where we would be ahead of the train when it started off in the morning, and concealed from the road until we chose to show ourselves. Then we settled down to wait.

My excitement that night was so great I couldn't sleep. The others, who had done this sort of thing many times before, wrapped themselves in their blankets and went quickly to sleep, but I lay awake and watched the stars, and wondered how I'd do tomorrow. I made all sorts of plans, trying to think everything through in advance so as not to be taken unprepared, and by the time the sky began to pale, I must have fought a hundred battles in my mind. Naturally, not one of them was like what really happened.

Dressing for battle is a very important thing, because what you are really doing is dressing to die. Every man wants to look his best when he comes into the presence of the Great Spirit, and every man has his own way of being prepared. Of course, most people use some sort of medicine to help them survive the day, but since no man's medicine is powerful all the time it's thought best to take everything into account before the fighting starts. Some do it in the manner of dressing and painting themselves, while others, who go into a fight more or less undressed, work their medicine spells as a form of blanket protection. Crazy Horse had his medicine stone behind his ear and the red-backed hawk atop his head, and as the light began to grow I could see he had painted the white lightning streak on his cheek. Others were quietly going about their own preparations, some tying up their ponies' tails with eagle feathers (your pony's tail is always tied up for war) and some painting their faces in their own special ways. I, who had never done this before, borrowed some red earth paint from Laughing Hawk and made lines from my eyes to my earlobes and three short lines on my chin, which is a sort of general way to paint for war. I decided that, when the day was over, I would work out a more definite design that would be my own. I might even have some special deed to illustrate, if I was lucky.

We all ate a little *wasna*—although I had my usual dry mouth, and trouble swallowing—and then Crazy Horse led us to the spot for the ambush. He told us that nobody was to fire, no matter what the excuse, until he gave the signal, which would be the cry of a wolf, twice repeated. He looked directly at me when he said it, and I remembered his talking to me about patience, and nodded to show I understood. Then he strung us out behind the ridge that bordered the road, and went off to take his position. We dismounted, and held our hands over our ponies' noses lest they whinny and give us away.

I don't remember the sunrise ever taking as long as it did that morning. The sky grew light until it seemed like noon, but still the sun didn't show itself over the rim of the hills. I felt that most of the day had already passed, but this was partly because I hadn't slept, and when I smelled the cooking fires of the wagon train my stomach began to rumble with hunger. Laughing Hawk, who was nearest to me, heard the sound and looked at me and smiled, and he ran his tongue over his lips and I could tell he was as anxious as I to get the action started. But still nothing happened; we could hear the clink of cooking utensils and the voices of the white men, and, because we couldn't see them, they seemed a lot closer than they really were. To me, they seemed to be just over the crest of the hill, and I couldn't understand why Crazy Horse was waiting so long to attack.

The reason was simple: they'd formed their wagons into a circle for the night, and he wanted to wait until they were once more strung out in line. I realized this when I heard the sounds of the horses being harnessed, the jangling of their equipment, and then the cries of the drivers and the creak of wheels as the wagons started off. At the same time, the signal came down the line for us to move closer to the ridge, and with my heart pounding in my chest I eased forward, tense as a rattlesnake. My pony's ears were up and the whites of his eyes were showing, and I clutched his soft nose, which fluttered with every breath. The creaking of the wheels became louder, and the shouts of the drivers were mixed with the cracking of whips, some of which sounded as loud as pistol shots. I had a moment of wondering if they were shots, and the battle had begun without my knowing it, but I was sure I hadn't heard the wolf-call signal, and I looked at Laughing Hawk to see what he thought. He was staring straight ahead, still licking his lips. Suddenly, over the crest of the hill in front of me appeared a big-brimmed black hat, a white face beneath it, and then a horse's head. The man's eyes, when he saw me, went as big and as white as two moons and his mouth fell open, showing a line of jagged teeth. Then he started to shout, and I raised my gun and fired, and through the smoke I saw him clutch his throat and fall. Things seem to happen very slowly at times like this, and I remember noticing, as he fell, that there was an arrow through his throat, which meant it hadn't been my shot that got him. Then I saw Lame Bear, one of the Dog warriors in charge of discipline, riding straight at me, his face snarled with fury, and before I could raise my hand he struck me across the face with his pony whip. I fell back, and he shouted, "You heard the order!"

"But he saw me!" I cried. "He was giving the alarm!"

Then I heard the wolf call, and many shots, and Lame Bear whirled and rode over the crest with the others. I flung myself on my pony and followed, still burning with shame and anger. I realized I'd gone against the order, but I'd had no way of knowing an arrow would cut the man down before he could cry out. My shooting had been instinct, not disobedience.

When I cleared the crest, I saw that the entire wagon train was in confusion. Some of the men were trying to get the wagons back in a circle, some were scrambling to get under the wagons and fire at us through the wheels, and some were trying to make barricades out of their packing cases. The first of our men had already reached the wagons and were firing directly into them, and then they rode off and more came in, forming a moving circle. When I got there a good many of the white men were dead or wounded, and those remaining were trying to fight their way into the trees on the other side of the road. They made it, only because our people were more interested in what was in the wagon train than they were in killing white men; if we'd wanted to, we could have rubbed out the entire lot. Those who got away fired at us only when we tried to chase them, and Crazy Horse gave the order we weren't to risk our lives any further. The Dog warriors saw to it he was obeyed.

We broke open the packing cases, and found all sorts of

things. There were blankets—good, heavy blankets, made of sheep's wool—there were bolts of colored cloth and barrels of flour, and in one case there were tools and cooking utensils made of real hard metal, not like the rusted tinny things they gave out at the agency. There were also guns and ammunition, and the Dog warriors took charge of that right away, to make sure there was an even distribution among us. We could scramble all we wanted for the other things, but the guns and ammunition were important.

There were also shirts and jackets, some taken from the men who'd just been killed, and when our men put them on they found the stink of white men's sweat was so unpleasant that they took them off again, and tied them to their gun barrels to dry in the wind. They rode around in circles laughing, and waving the shirts to make them dry faster.

There was good reason for laughter, too, because we had captured many goods and horses, and hadn't lost a man. Only two were wounded, neither badly, and we were far richer than when we started out. Richer in the things that counted, because beyond the guns and ammunition we had metal, which could be hammered into weapons such as bullets and lance tips and arrowheads. We scoured the ground for empty shell cases, and picked up every bit of metal we could find, even stripping the rims off the wagon wheels. The white men's horseshoes would, in time, be used for arrowheads, but right now it was most important to keep their horses in good shape, for bringing home the goods. It makes you feel happy when you come into luck like this, and you laugh at things you wouldn't usually think are funny.

My happiness, of course, was dimmed by the ugly way the day had started, with Lame Bear lashing me across the face. I knew that the warriors—the *akicita* members—were charged with keeping discipline, and I knew how I'd erred, but I felt I hadn't deserved the disgrace of being lashed like a criminal. I thought of going to Lame Bear to explain, but I'd already told him why I'd fired, and he hadn't been impressed. Then I thought I might tell Crazy Horse, because he had been so direct in his warning to me. I found him off to one side, quietly watching the others cavort around the wreckage of the wagons. I said nothing as I approached, and waited for him to address me.

"I know," he said, without looking at me. "I was told."

"Did he tell you why?" I asked.

"There is no why," said Crazy Horse.

"I thought it was the only thing to do."

"You aren't supposed to think. That's what orders are for."

There was nothing I could reply to this, so I simply said, "I hear you."

"We have lost many good men who acted on their own," he went on, after a moment. "Lakotas are so eager to show their courage they cannot wait; they always want to charge off alone."

"I didn't . . ." I began, but he kept on talking.

"We can no longer afford to lose men like that. The white men are too many, and we are growing few. The only thing we can do is always act together, and not try for single feats of bravery." I thought of my own desire to prove myself, as he continued, "Bravery alone means nothing, because a corpse

is neither cowardly nor brave. To stay alive we must act together, and forget our own desires. Otherwise, we're lost
before we start."

"I hear you," I said, again.

"Today, it made no difference. Another day, it might have
been the difference between defeat and victory."

"I understand."

"Then nothing has been wasted."

The sun was now high, and the day was hot, and flies were
beginning to swarm around the corpses. Crazy Horse looked
at the sky for a moment, then said, "We should be far from
here by night. We can't risk running into Bluecoats."

We packed the goods onto the horses, ate some food from
the wagons, then set them afire and started off. We traveled
all that day, heading slowly home, and that night we camped
among the trees, far from the white men and their roads. I
slept like a child hanging in its cradle board; a hundred
thunderstorms could not have wakened me.

Next morning, as though to show he still had trust in me,
Crazy Horse sent me out as one of the advance scouts. I rode
to meet the incoming scout, exchanged a greeting as we
passed, then went on to search the country on one side of our
route. The air was still cool, and the trees made a gentle
sighing in the wind, and I remembered my first trip into the
Paha Sapa to ask the Spirit what to do. I wondered if I'd
truly had the answer, and if my course was right, but I could
think of nothing else that made sense and finally concluded
this was it. I would just have to realize patience is required,
as well as bravery.

I came to a crest and looked to where the *Paha Sapa* rose, dark and mysterious, into the base of a line of thunderclouds. The clouds seemed an extension of the mountains, reaching high into the sky, and I could see small flicks of lightning, like the tongues of snakes. I was so caught up in the sight that it was a while before my eyes picked out a distant road, along which crawled a line of wagons. My heart jumped, and I began to see in my mind another rousing fight, and more captured goods, and a chance to redeem myself with glory. Then I saw, ahead of the white wagon tops, a long dark line and a colored flag, and I realized the train was escorted by a heavy force of soldiers. More soberly, I rode back and reported to Crazy Horse, and he and the others followed me to the spot and looked. For a long time no one spoke, and I could see Crazy Horse counting up the odds against us. They were impossible, but he couldn't take his eyes off the column, and for a long time we watched in silence as it threaded its way toward the holy mountains. Then, almost as though he didn't want to see the end, Crazy Horse pulled away from the crest and headed back toward home.

When we arrived, Worm had bad news for us. (I should explain that Crazy Horse's father had changed his name to Worm when he gave his own name to his son. It was a common thing to change names like that, and it caused less confusion than you might think.) Worm was still revered as a holy man, and although he was old, and no longer had the dash of a warrior, he was highly regarded among the Big Bellies, as the older chiefs were called. Generally speaking, the Big Bellies made the policy decisions, and the warriors carried them out. The women and children did as they were told. Worm said that while we were gone messengers had come with the news that the white men wanted to buy the *Paha Sapa,* and were sending men out to the agencies to make the arrangements. At first, Crazy Horse didn't understand.

"What do you mean, buy the *Paha Sapa?*" he asked. "They said it is ours forever."

"Now they want to buy it," his father replied. "They are bringing many gifts."

Crazy Horse snorted. "Not for me."

"Nor me. But it means we must all be warriors again. Remember what I said: One does not go to a hilltop for water, or to a white man for the truth."

"I remember," said Crazy Horse. "Those are words I never forget."

He did forget them, but that's another story. It cost him his life.

6

It was early in the Moon-of-the-Calves-Growing-Hair, which the white men call September, that messengers arrived from the Red Cloud agency, trying to induce Crazy Horse to come to the council on the *Paha Sapa*. There were about a hundred Loaf-About-the-Forts in the party, bringing travois loaded with gifts, and they almost ran into trouble before they could deliver the message. Some Minneconjoux were in our camp, and they looked on the Loafers as little better than traitors. They wanted to charge them and scatter them in a gesture of contempt, but Crazy Horse, although he looked with a cold eye on the Loafers and their gifts, prevented any violence. He took the spokesmen into the council lodge, and invited them to speak. Outside, people gathered around to listen. Not much could be heard as the pipe was filled with red willow bark, lighted with a fire stick, then offered to the sky, the earth, and the four great directions. I could see in my mind what was happening, and I knew the messengers were nervous.

One of the Loafers from the party sidled up to where I was standing, and edged closer to speak. His blanket was thin and ragged, and the skin hung loosely on his bones, and remembering my father I felt pity for him. From beneath his blanket he brought out a bag of real tobacco, and offered it to me. I was tempted, but I refused it.

"I have more," he said, in a clogged voice. "At Red Cloud there is plenty of tobacco."

"And anything else?" I asked. It was rude, because I knew the answer, but I disliked his trying to paint a good picture.

"You see the gifts we brought," he replied. "There are all these and more, for those who come in."

"I know all about that," I told him. "My parents died there last winter."

He withdrew the bag, which he'd been holding out, and put it beneath his blanket. For a few moments he was quiet, and then he coughed and said, "I hear you have buffalo meat here. Fresh buffalo meat. Is that true?"

I was trying to listen to what was going on inside, and his talking irritated me. "No," I said, shortly.

After a pause, he said, "Any dried?"

"Yes," I said, still trying to listen.

He looked around, and his red eyes lit on one of the travois loaded with gifts. "It's a long time since I tasted buffalo," he said, at last. "Perhaps if I were to . . ."

"Why do you come to me for food?" I cut in. "Go to the women, and let them feed you."

"They refused," he replied. "I asked, but they said no." He coughed again.

This Loafer was making me angry because he was forcing me to be rude, and I felt that in some way I was being rude to my father. I told myself my father wouldn't have come begging like this, but I wasn't sure, knowing what life at the agency had done to his pride. I was about to get some meat for him when a great babble of angry muttering came from the lodge, as though it were suddenly filled with swarming bees. There were grunts and coughs and the stamping of feet, and I could sense that the matter of the *Paha Sapa* had just been brought up. This was confirmed when I heard the voice of one of the Loafers' spokesmen protesting: "This land is lost anyway. It is full of white men, and more are coming every day. They have soldiers, and they have far-shooting wagon guns. The only sensible thing is to come and touch the pen to the treaty, and then collect the gifts."

"What gifts?" I heard Crazy Horse ask, quietly. "What gifts are worth the sacred hills?"

"Money," the Loafer replied. "White men's money. It will buy anything you need for many years to come."

There was silence, and then Crazy Horse was talking again. He spoke so softly that I had to lean forward to hear, and all I caught were the words, ". . . sky, or the four great directions. One does not sell the earth upon which people walk."

That was all. Nobody spoke, and after a while there was a shuffling of feet, and people began to come out of the lodge. Their faces held no expression, but I could see in the eyes of some of the Loafers a sort of tortured look; they'd cast their lot with the white men, but the hearts of many of them were still with Crazy Horse. I learned later that Sitting Bull, the Hunkpapa chief and medicine man, had the same reaction as Crazy Horse: when the half-breed Louis Richard read the white men's proposal to him, Sitting Bull said, "I want you to go and tell the Great Father that I do not want to sell any land to the Government." Then he picked up some dust, and let it sift through his fingers, and went on, "Not even so much as this."

But there were many who were at least willing to talk; on the grounds that nothing could be lost by talking, and there were often many good gifts at the encampment when a treaty was being discussed. Already, the Great Father had given a silver-trimmed rifle to Red Cloud in thanks for his work at the agency, and young Sitting Bull, Little Wound's nephew whom the whites called "The Good" because of his beating us back at the flagpole trouble, had received a rifle trimmed in gold. The whites were trying hard to show that good things happened to those who worked with them, and if you took only those two examples it was indeed so.

When the Loafers had gone, there was silence in the camp. Crazy Horse did not then know that he and Sitting Bull were the only two chiefs of importance who had refused to attend the meeting; all he knew was he wanted nothing to do with it. But he did want to know what went on, and who might speak for selling the hills, so he decided to move closer to the council grounds and then send observers down, with messengers to come back each day and tell him what had happened. The chief observer was Little Big Man, a warrior friend with whom he had shared a lot of fighting in the early days, and one he knew would not be tempted by any of the white men's offerings. In fact, Little Big Man was, if anything, almost too hostile to the whites to be a good observer, but Crazy Horse felt that one way or another he could be kept under control. The fact that he was wrong didn't come out until later, when Little Big Man almost turned the meeting into a massacre. (And, on the subject of Little Big Man, there seems to have been a white adopted by the Cheyennes who called himself by that name, and the two should not be confused.) As messengers, Crazy Horse chose Laughing Hawk and me, with the thought that any experience we had with the whites would stand us in good stead later on. We all knew the whites were here to stay, although some of us didn't care to admit it. Most felt that if we could just stay out of their way, everything would be all right. It had always seemed there was enough land for all, but now we were beginning to wonder. It was not a good thought, and people faced it in different ways. Some, like the Loafers, accepted defeat as a fact; others, like Sitting Bull and Crazy Horse, decided to fight for their rights. As for me, I was determined to fight to the end. As I saw it, that was all there was left.

The meeting was held on the White River, between the Red Cloud and Spotted Tail agencies, and I will never forget the sight as Little Big Man, Laughing Hawk, and I rode down from the bluffs. The whole plain, as far as the eye could see, was crowded with Indians—not only Lakotas, but Cheyennes and Arapahos as well—and it seemed that every tribe from the Missouri River to the Bighorn Mountains had gathered to show the whites what they had to deal with. Little Big Man was riding a large, gray American horse, which made him seem taller than he was, and I remember the look that came into his eyes as he surveyed the herds of ponies, the hundreds of lodges, and the many thousand warriors. He had wide cheekbones, which made his eyes seem sunk deep in his head, but there was a glint in them that showed very clearly what he was thinking. He was using his warrior's judgment of what would happen if all these people should turn on the white men at one time, and he was reveling in the joy of the imagined massacre. His face was cold, and no white man could have told what he was thinking, but to me it was as if he were speaking out loud.

On the day of the meeting, the whites gathered near a cottonwood tree in the middle of the plain. The sun was hot, and they rigged a sort of open-sided tent of canvas, to give their people shade and also to give them a little dignity, in

96

the face of all the swarming Indians. Their people sat on chairs, stiffly and without expression, probably wondering what was going to happen next. Among their number were a Senator named Allison, a religious man named Hinman, General Terry of the pony soldiers, and a trader from Fort Laramie named Collins. There were also men who wrote on paper, and a few women, although what they were there for no one could tell. A hundred and more pony soldiers from Fort Robinson rode up and formed in lines behind the tent. Their horses were nervous in the presence of so many of us, and my mind went back to the time of the flagpole trouble. That all seemed long ago, and unimportant. I looked for the young blond soldier I had brushed with, but couldn't find him. I was not close, but I could smell the familiar stink of white men's sweat. I wondered how they stood it.

There was a short wait, and then the creaking of a wagon, and Spotted Tail rode in from his agency. He was a Brulé, and even if he hadn't been dressed in all his feathers he would have been impressive. He had a large, strong jaw, and a mouth that was as big as a bear's but somehow gentle, and his heavy-lidded eyes showed wisdom and strength. His face was one that could be all things but never weak, and the main thing you felt was that you never wanted to cross his path in anger. Even Red Cloud, who had once been thought so powerful, had lost to Spotted Tail in the matter of where to hold the meeting; and possibly because of this, Red Cloud was not there the first day. The Bad Face, as he did so often, said he'd hold aside a while, and see.

A few more chiefs came slowly into the council circle, but

97

nobody said anything, and there was no sign that the meeting was ready to begin. The white people shifted in their chairs and looked about them, and one or two took out handkerchiefs and wiped their faces. The women fanned themselves with what looked like little bits of bone, which opened and closed. Suddenly there was a pounding of hooves, and shots, and howling, and a band of painted, feathered warriors came charging at the council shelter. The troopers reined their horses tight and slid their hands toward their guns, and the people in the shelter stiffened and grasped the sides of their chairs, and the warriors rode straight at them, still shooting their rifles in the air, and then at the last moment broke, spread out, and trotted into a line behind the troopers. I could see a few of the warriors grinning behind the soldiers' backs, at the fright they had given the whites. Then another band came charging up, and another, until the whole council area was ringed with armed and painted warriors. As more arrived their lines got deeper, until not only the white people in their shelter but also their pony soldiers might as well have been our prisoners. The air was full of dust, and the snorting and stamping of the ponies, and the paint on the warriors' faces made their eyes seem unusually large and white. For me, it was as exciting as anything I'd ever seen; for the whites, it must have been a horror. I almost felt pity for them, until I remembered why they were there.

Then a silence settled down, and the council chiefs came slowly out of the crowd, walking in single file. They sat themselves with Spotted Tail, in a half circle facing the whites, and lit the long-stemmed pipe to begin the parley. The pipe was offered to the sky, the earth, and the four great directions, and then passed around, and when that was done the religion man, Hinman, got up and offered a prayer to their Great Spirit. During my time at the agency I learned enough of their language to know what he was saying, and it went something like this: "Bless, O Lord, Thy servants gathered here, and bless also their mission, that Thy Word may be spread among the heathen, and their eyes opened unto the True Light. Bless also these heathens, that the scales may fall from their eyes and they may, by sharing with us Thy servants the bounteous lands where Thou hast allowed them to dwell, enter into the true Kingdom of the Brotherhood of Man. Make not their hearts hard to us, who would help them, but make them see the True Love we bring in Thy name. Amen."

Laughing Hawk, who was standing next to me, leaned to my ear and said. "What is he saying?"

I thought for a moment, trying to digest what I'd heard, and finally I told him, "He wants us all to be brothers."

Laughing Hawk considered this. "A lot of talk for an old idea," he said, at last.

Then Allison, the Council Chief, stood up. He wore a black suit, and across the front of his vest was a chain of the yellow metal that was the root of all the trouble. The tooth of an elk hung from the chain, and for a moment I wondered if he was a hunter. Then I knew that was impossible; some hunter must have given it to him, and he wore it not knowing that elks' teeth are used only to decorate women's dresses, and are not for men. If he wanted to impress us he should have worn a bear's claw, or wolf's tooth, on his chain. It made me smile at how ignorant he was, and I wondered if this was the best man the Great Father could find to make a treaty with us. It seemed it was either the soldiers, who tried to kill us, or men like this, who even in the smallest things were wrong. But when he started to talk, I could hardly believe what I was hearing. What he suggested was that we *loan* him the *Paha Sapa*, so that the miners could dig in it until they'd taken out all the yellow metal, and then, he said, the hills would be given back to us to do with as we wanted. While this was being translated, Spotted Tail's face took on an expression of disbelief, as though he were being asked to put on a woman's dress. It was a moment before he spoke.

"Would you loan me a team of mules that way?" he said, at last. "Even for money, would you let me use something, and then give it back when it was worthless?"

"That is my proposal," Allison replied. "You will be paid a fair and just sum for their use." The thought of Worm's "One does not go to a hilltop for water, or to a white man for the truth" went through my mind, while Allison went on that it would be very hard for the Government to keep the men out of the *Paha Sapa* because there were so many who wanted to go in, and to me this meant that they either could not, or did not want to, control their own people.

In either case, what kind of government was this for us to be dealing with? But his next suggestion was so wild that it became clear he didn't know what he was talking about. He said that the Powder River country out to the Bighorn Mountains, which was our last good hunting country, *didn't seem much use to us,* and the white men would like to take that over as well! While that was being translated, a silence as thick as night spread through the onlookers, and before anyone could react there came a thumping of hooves and Red Dog rode up, the dust swirling around his pony's hooves as he stopped.

"I bring a message from Chief Red Cloud!" he called out, in a loud voice. "A message from Chief Red Cloud!"

"What is it?" Allison asked, with faint irritation.

"Chief Red Cloud asks that the council be put off for seven days, so that all the chiefs may confer among themselves on the white men's proposals. Chief Red Cloud says these are not decisions that should be made quickly." It would seem that, since Red Cloud hadn't yet heard the white men's proposals, he had guessed they'd be outrageous, and knew more time would be needed. Allison turned, and spoke in a low voice to the other whites. Then he turned back, and on his face were unmistakable signs of relief.

"You may have three days," he said. "We will meet here again three days from now." He had sensed the ugly mood that had been growing, and was glad for the chance to let it cool down.

Little Big Man, Laughing Hawk, and I rode back to Crazy Horse with the news, and he took it without surprise. He called a meeting in the council lodge, and when the pipe had been smoked Litle Big Man repeated what we'd heard. "I say kill the whites," he concluded. "Rub them out, and get it over with."

"No good will come of that," said Crazy Horse. "They'll always send out more."

"Then kill anyone who wants to sell," Bear Brains suggested. "If we cannot kill whites, then kill those who would act for them. It will serve just as well."

"It's best we shouldn't start the killing," said Crazy Horse. "That only leads to more."

"Would you let them sell the land?" asked Little Big Man.

"I, myself, would never sell," Crazy Horse replied. "I do not believe you can sell the land any more than you can the sky. All I ask is to be let alone. If they try to take the land from me, then I will fight. If they leave me alone, I will leave them alone. There was a time when killing made me feel good, but that was long ago. When my daughter died I killed many white men for revenge, but the revenge was hollow because it didn't bring her back. It just made one more death."

"And one less white man," said Little Big Man.

Crazy Horse looked at him quietly. "There will always be white men," he said.

"Not if I could have my way."

"It does no good to hide from facts. They are here. The best we can do is keep away."

He then told us to go back to the council grounds, and find out what the chiefs were saying. With three days before the next meeting there was sure to be a lot of discussion, and he wanted to know how the others felt. We left next morning, and I had the strange feeling I was going over a waterfall. I didn't know what would happen next, but I had a murky fear it would be bad.

What we found out was what we suspected: the chiefs were divided on how to reply. Not one favored giving up the Powder River country, but on the matter of the *Paha Sapa* there was much discussion. Some said the land was lost anyway and we should take what money we could get, while others denied it was lost and said they'd fight anyone who tried to come in. Even among those who would take money there was no agreement; Red Cloud thought six million dollars plus rations for the next seven generations sounded like a fair price, while Spotted Tail had different ideas, and other chiefs had theirs. When time for the next meeting came, there still was no agreement.

I had not seen Little Big Man since the day after we returned to the council grounds. He'd had a wild look in his eye that reminded me of a pony in a thunderstorm, and he seemed not to be listening to what went on around him; then he vanished. Laughing Hawk, who rode back to Crazy Horse with the latest news, hadn't seen him either, so that meant he was somewhere around the encampment, but doing what we couldn't say. With twenty thousand Indians in the area, it was impossible to seek out a single one. We were both uneasy, but couldn't tell exactly why.

The day of the second meeting was hot like the first, although the smoky sky of summer had given way to the clearer blue of autumn. The whites came riding in from Fort Robinson in an Army ambulance, and with more troopers than the first time, and they arranged themselves the way they had before. This time Red Cloud was present, and also Spotted Tail and the chiefs of the Minneconjou, No Bows, Hunkpapa, Blackfoot, Two Kettle, and Yanktonnais tribes, but before they could start the parley, there came the same rush of mounted warriors from the hills, then another, and a third, until there was the ring of warriors around the council ground. There were some new ones this time, from the wilder tribes to the north, and where the mood had been almost festive the first time, now it was angry, because the word had gone into the hills about the whites' demands. Some rode around, singing and firing their rifles, while others quietly took position behind the troopers, in case of trouble. As before there were many thousands of Indians surrounding about two hundred whites.

Then Red Cloud, Spotted Tail, and the other council chiefs sat down and smoked, and tried to agree among themselves who would speak up first. Because of the differences among them this was hard to decide; and nobody wanted to start, since there was a rumor the hostiles would kill whoever spoke up for selling the *Paha Sapa*. Even Red Cloud and Spotted Tail, powerful chiefs in their own right, held back from speaking first. They were, in one way, as much prisoners of the Indians as were the whites. They sat, and smoked, and talked, while the white men waited in the

shelter of their tent. The sun climbed slowly in the sky, until
it was directly overhead.

Suddenly, there was a stir among the circling warriors;
they parted, and through their ranks came Little Big Man,
riding his gray horse and waving his Winchester and a belt
of shells. He had clearly been doing a medicine dance; he
was wearing nothing but his breechcloth and had fresh blood
running down his chest, from where he'd torn his flesh with
the thongs. He was painted for battle and his eyes were wild,
and he charged toward the council tent, shouting that he'd
kill the men who tried to steal his land and those who would
sell it. He stopped short of the tent, and his horse's dancing
hooves kicked up dust that sifted over the terrified whites.
There was silence, while everyone held their breath and
waited for the first shot. The troopers, as well as the white
council people, were the color of ashes, and the Indians were
like blocks of stone, their guns held ready. I felt my mouth
go dry, as before battle, and the silence seemed without
end. Then, Young-Man-Afraid-of-His-Horse came forward,
quietly, and with a few *akicita* warriors he edged Little Big
Man back from the tent. Then, addressing all those who held
their guns ready, he told them to go to their lodges until their
heads had cooled. It was the calm way he spoke that made the
effect; if he'd shouted, or been violent in any way, the shooting would have started. There was a moment as tense as the
pause before a bowstring is released, and the whole picture
was frozen in my mind: the whites, pale as death and not
daring to breathe; the council chiefs, sitting motionless on

the ground, with Spotted Tail clutching the long-stemmed pipe; and the surging, silent circle of warriors, rifles pointed toward the whites and their fingers on the triggers.

Behind that circle was another, and another, until the council area seemed no bigger than a leaf in a lake of feathered warriors. But the calm of Young-Man-Afraid spread outward through the lake, and slowly the tension relaxed. One or two of the warriors turned their ponies' heads and edged away, and that started a general movement. Even Little Big Man, although still breathing heavily, had lost the peak of his rage, and he sensed the moment for action had gone. It was like the slow settling of a wounded buffalo, who one moment is running at a gallop, then loses speed, stops, goes to his knees, and topples over. Once the speed is lost, it never comes back.

When the crowd of warriors had thinned, the whites sprang from their chairs, hurried into the Army ambulance, and drove away, escorted by the sweating troopers. They never came back to the council tent, and held their later meetings with the twenty agency chiefs inside the stockade at Red Cloud.

When we reported to Crazy Horse, he said, "That ends it. We might as well go home." He knew what was later confirmed by messengers: the talks would break down, and the whites would return to Washington, more determined than ever to take the *Paha Sapa* by force.

7

The time had come to start preparing for winter, which meant moving camp, hunting, and gathering food and skins for the coming cold months. My thoughts kept turning to Lashuka, and wondering if she'd finally given in to Running Deer or some other suitor, and I decided that as soon as my duties let me, I'd visit Two Moon's camp and see how she was. So much had been happening that my mind had been taken away from her, and only at night would I think, with a sort of aching sadness, of her eyes and her voice and the smell of sweet grass about her. I would remember how she'd opened up and talked to me the way no girl had ever done before, and I would renew my resolve to get her grandmother's consent. Provided it wasn't too late.

This fear kept gnawing at my innards, because she'd told me she couldn't wait forever, and it already seemed that long since I'd seen her. It's strange that something can leave your mind and then come back more strongly than before, but that's what happened with me; when I wasn't thinking of her I was happy, but the moment I let my thoughts rest on her I became tortured and miserable, and would have walked barefoot over coals if it would have got her for me. I decided that at the next medicine dance I would test my courage by piercing my flesh with the thongs, and straining at them until they tore out. That sort of thing renews a man's heart, and makes him strong,

Crazy Horse's camp was now about a hundred lodges strong, including the Minneconjoux and some people Black Elk had brought along. The day before we moved, the herald went about the camp, announcing that all lodges should be down and packed the following morning, and that the members of the Fox *akicita* would be in charge of the moving. I was glad it wouldn't be the Dog warriors again, because I still felt the sting of Lame Bear's quirt across my face, and felt a burn of shame whenever I saw him. Now he would be just another Oglala like the rest, and the Fox

108

warriors would be the ones to be obeyed. I longed for the day when I would be asked to join one of the *akicitas*, but I had to admit that so far I'd done little to deserve it. You don't make a name as a warrior by carrying messages.

I should explain Crazy Horse's unusual position in the camp. He had once been one of the big chiefs, wearing the hair shirt of a bighorn sheep as his sign of honor, but after the man named No Water had shot him about a woman (Crazy Horse had, in effect, run away with No Water's wife), Crazy Horse chased No Water and his friends out of camp, and in that way violated his oath as a shirt-wearer. The Big Bellies stripped him of his shirt, and forbade him to smoke anything but a short-stemmed pipe, but his medicine was still so strong, and the people believed in him so firmly, that he remained the one they listened to, and they were known as Crazy Horse's people. He had the power of a Big Belly, but none of the trappings. He remained "Our Strange Man," who could never be harmed except by one of his own people. That had been part of his vision, and it was borne out by the fact that Little Big Man had pinned his arms just as No Water shot him in the face. Little Big Man had been trying to prevent the fight, but the result had nearly been the death of Crazy Horse. And when he finally did die, Little Big Man was again holding his arms. By that time Little Big Man, the white-hater, was an agency policeman.

The Crow Owners *akicita* had been in charge of camp discipline the day before we moved, and they went off duty, and the Foxes took over. The chief herald gathered the Foxes together and gave them their instructions, although they knew them by heart. He told them they should make all people obey them and make the people stay in their proper places. They were authorized to pony-whip any offenders, or punish them in any way they thought best, which included shooting their horses, killing their dogs, breaking their guns or their bows, or shredding their clothing. They were allowed to inflict any punishment, short of death. While these instructions were going on the women were loading the travois and the pack animals, and then the procession started: the Big Bellies first, then their herald, then the Fox warriors, then the ordinary people and the baggage train, then the pony herd and the children. The Fox warriors rode back and forth, keeping order along the line and herding stragglers into position, and one group of them rode rear guard, to make sure no Crows or Pawnees came up from behind. Our line was so long that a raid could be made on our rear without those in front being aware of it.

This way we rode all day, our travois poles cutting deep furrows in the earth. The Big Bellies selected a campsite for the night; the heralds passed the word, and the lodges were set up in the standard open circle, each with its opening facing the east. The fire carriers distributed their coals, the cooking fires were lighted, and we settled down. It had been a long day and a dull one, with no sign of action anywhere. Crazy Horse seemed in another world, lost in his thoughts, and the only sounds in his lodge came from Black Shawl, his wife, who had developed a cough.

Next day the Dog warriors were in charge, and we started off as before. In the middle of the morning, a scout came riding back with the news that he'd seen a herd of buffalo far ahead, and the excitement that went through our people was like a flash of lightning. It wasn't a big herd, he said, but any buffalo was good news, and we right away started preparing for the hunt. The heralds passed the word for everyone to sharpen their knives and arrows—an unnecessary instruction, in this case, but heralds like to hear themselves talk—and when we approached the ridge beyond which the buffalo were grazing we broke out of the traveling formation, and arranged ourselves for the hunt. The Dog warriors rode ahead, in a line twenty abreast, to keep anyone from rushing forward and frightening the herd, and the rash hunter who tried to get around them would have been knocked spinning from his horse. Behind the Dogs, riding five abreast, were the hunters, stripped to the breechcloth and riding their fastest ponies, and I was in this group, in the sixth rank from the front. My quiver, full of arrows, was slung over my left shoulder, and the bow in my right hand was slippery with sweat. I wiped it, and then my hand, on my breechcloth, and waited for the next order. Behind us hunters were the old men and the women and children, holding back and being as quiet as they could. One boy of about twelve ducked away from his mother and ran toward the ridge, ignoring her calls, and a Dog warrior saw him, veered out of line, and with one vicious cut of his quirt slashed him to the ground. The boy lay, stunned and trying not to weep, while his mother ran up, pulled him to his feet, and dragged him to the rear. The Dog warrior, I saw as he trotted back into formation, was Lame Bear.

One of the Big Bellies now went among the hunters, selecting those who would do the killing for the old people. It was an honor to be chosen for this, because only the very best were selected. It's every man for himself in a hunt, and a man gets to keep whatever he has killed, but since there are many who are too old or too sick to hunt, some care must be taken of them, and that is how it's done. The good hunters can always find food, but the old people must depend on someone else. It is a good system, but it's another reason some people don't like to get old. They'd rather do their own hunting than depend on others, and rather die in glory than wither away in old age.

When we topped the rise, we saw the herd. It may not have been a large one, but it was more buffalo than I had seen in one place before. They were grazing quietly, their breath making a faint snuffling noise as they chomped the grass, and the old bulls were on the outside, to protect the cows and calves from the wolves that always follow. We were downwind so they didn't smell us, and too far away for their small eyes, sunk in their woolly heads, to make out what we were. We split into two groups and circled the herd, and when we had them between us, we shouted "Hoka hey!" and charged in. For a moment they didn't see us, and then their tails went up and they began to move, first one way and then another, trying to escape. We bore in among them, past the old bulls to get to the younger ones, and soon came the first cry of "Yahoo!" as a hunter scored a kill. It was followed by another, and then another, and then the thunder of hooves and the bawling of the animals drowned out all other sounds.

Through the press of black, surging humps I rode alongside a running yearling, pulled my bowstring back as far as I could, and sent an arrow into his left shoulder. It went up to the feathers but he didn't slow down, and I shot another, this time almost touching the tip to his hide before I let go. It vanished, passing all the way through without hitting bone, and he began to wobble, and blood came out of his nose, and then he went to his knees and was down. I shouted, "Yahoo!" so loud it made my throat hurt, and I rode after another. In all, I brought down three buffalo before they scattered away from us, and when I looked around, I saw that the plain was littered with dead and dying animals. We had done well.

Then the women and children rushed up, the women making the trilling noise of joy and the children leaping and shouting and begging pieces of raw liver and gut, as the carcasses were opened and the hides peeled back. Each hunter could tell his own kill from the markings on his arrows, and I had a long job ahead of me butchering those I had shot. But my heart was glad because I'd done well, and in the end two women came and helped me, so it wasn't tiresome. I thought, once, how much better it would be if it were Lashuka who was helping me, but I put that out of my mind as an ungrateful thought, almost a greedy one. When you

113

have any happiness at all, it's not a good thing to ask for more.

When the butchering was done, the strips of red meat were wrapped in layers of hide and hung across the horses' backs, and fastened with pieces of sinew and hide. The marrow bones were lashed on top, and the entrails that could later be used were wrapped in hide to be taken back and cured. (The stomach, for instance, is useful for making soup; you put the water and meat in it with herbs and turnips and hot stones, and it is a self-contained cooker.) I cut two long rib bones from one of my carcasses, and gave them to the boy Lame Bear had whipped, so he could make them into a sled when the snow fell. His face bore a big welt, and his eyes were like those of an antelope, but my present cheered him a little, and he thanked me. His mother said nothing, but her face thanked me even more.

Some of the women had already started to set up camp, and had cut long poles and forked sticks to make drying racks for the meat. They saved the leaves and spread them out on the ground, and when the hunters got back they unloaded the meat and piled it on the leaves. Then the women set about cutting it into small pieces, the thickness of a man's hand, and hanging it on the racks. Cooking fires were lighted, and by the time night fell, a fine feast was in progress. The first and best cuts of meat were taken to the leaders of the hunt, who had gathered in the council lodge, and there was much singing and thanks and praise all around. Then, when the leaders had eaten their fill, the heralds went around calling for everybody else to come and get some meat, and there followed general eating, singing, and laughter. A drum was brought out, and people began to dance and sing songs in praise of themselves, each other, and the Dog warriors. I wondered if Lame Bear was going to sing a song in praise of himself for whipping a twelve-year-old boy, but he didn't seem to think it that important. It's one thing to whip a man who disobeys orders, and it's quite another thing to whip a child. We used to say that the white men loved their horses and whipped their children, while we did just the other way around, and I think, all things considered, our system was better. Lame Bear was what we called a savage, and I guess there's one in every group.

The children had a game they used to play whenever there was a good hunt. It was a sort of mimic war game, and they would go off from the camp and make a village of grass tepees for themselves, after which they'd hold a council, and one would act as advisor and tell the others to raid our camp and steal some meat. So the others would crawl on their bellies toward the camp (this was usually after the sun went down) and try to get to the meat racks without being seen by the women. If it wasn't little boys trying to steal the meat it was the dogs, or, in the daytime, the magpies and crows and other birds, so the women were always on the alert. They had sticks and clubs, to keep the predators away. If a boy could sneak up and get a piece of meat and bring it back to his "village," that counted as a coup, and he could boast about it when they all got together later. Sometimes the women, knowing what was going on, would let a boy make off with a small piece of meat, but usually they chased them away. They were never angry, though, because it gave the boys something to do while the men were singing and dancing, and it was good training for later life. Still, their main thought was to protect the meat, without which we all would die.

Next day, while the women were staking out the hides and rubbing them with bits of brains and suet to soften them for curing, the older men went out to the hunting ground and scoured the earth for arrowheads. They picked up everything they found that could be used again, and, as a last gesture of thanks to the buffalo, they turned the whitening skulls toward the west, and the setting sun.

8

We made winter camp along the Tongue River, near where the Thieves' Road came into the *Paha Sapa* from the north, and where we could make raids on the miners when spring came. There were many cottonwood trees in the area, and the women cut poles to make a corral for the ponies, using the bark of the trees for fodder. The ponies liked it, and they stayed fat longer than they would have on just grass. We needed a strong corral, because the Crows had been coming south of the Yellowstone on horse raids, and you never knew when or where they were going to strike. The Crows made a big thing of horse stealing, whereas we did it only when we needed the horses. We and the Cheyennes thought of ourselves as warriors above everything else, and I think most people will agree we were. Long ago, before they had guns, the Cheyennes were a peaceable people and others took advantage of them, so when they got guns they vowed to be more warlike than anyone else, and they succeeded. (I talk here as though I'd been born a Lakota instead of a Cheyenne, but I lived with the Oglalas so much I've come to think of myself as one—except when I'm with the Cheyennes. Then I revert.)

The snow that winter was so heavy it was hard for anyone to go anywhere, and I never got to make my visit to Lashuka. Each time I was about to start a howling blizzard struck, and the snow piled up until some of the lodges were almost covered. The cold was so sharp it bit deep into your bones, like a wolf gnawing at you, and only those with the heaviest furs could stay outside for long. So, Laughing Hawk and I passed the time making arrows, and lances, and any other weapons we could think of, and endlessly sharpening those we already had. We made rawhide lariats and quirts and extra quivers, and I made a shield of buffalo hide, stretched over a wooden frame and decorated with feathers and a drawing of an elk's head. More than anything I wanted a whistle made from the wing bone of an eagle, which warriors use in battle, but they were not easy to get and those who had them wanted a lot in trade. Of course, if I'd had better luck catching my eagle . . . but there was no point thinking that way. One day I'd have one, and in the meantime I made arrows and bullets, and sharpened my knife, and thought about Lashuka. It's strange, when you think about it, how someone whom you really know very slightly can take charge of your whole life. I had seen Lashuka only a few times, but everything I did now centered around her, and how it might affect our later life together. The deeds to impress her grandmother were only the first step; my growing determination to fight the white men stemmed from the fact that I wanted the land for Lashuka and me, and everything centered around her. Without her, I felt the future was just a gaping void, and while this wasn't a very intelligent feeling, or a very mature one, I couldn't help it; she was as much a part of me as my arms and legs.

In January, the Moon-of-Frost-in-the-Lodge, a messenger from the Red Cloud agency made his way through the snow on horseback, bringing word that any Indians not on the reservation by the end of that month would be considered hostile, and treated as such. In other words, soldiers would be sent out against them. The foolishness of this order was shown by the fact that it had taken the messenger almost a full moon to reach us, and he himself was unable to get back to Red Cloud until long after the time had run out. To move a camp of a hundred or more lodges, with women and children and weakened ponies, was impossible. Crazy Horse

119

told him quietly that this was our country and we would do as we pleased, and whatever we did it would not be before the snow melted and there was grass for the ponies. The messenger went away knowing, as he had known when he brought the summons, that the result could only be war. The men in Washington had already decided that.

Next month, the Moon-of-the-Dark-Red-Calf, there came a sudden thaw; the air turned soft and the sky was clear, and the snow ran off in torrents of water. The black earth showed through, and it seemed that the winter was done. There were those who remembered the word from Red Cloud, and decided it would be better to get back to the agency late than stay out and be chased by the soldiers, and they held a council with Crazy Horse, to ask what he thought. He was frank with them.

"I cannot hold anyone here," he said. "It is for each man to listen to his own heart, and act as he thinks best."

Black Elk was troubled. "My heart tells me to stay here," he said, "but my mind tells me to go in. With the Bluecoats coming against us, it will be bad."

"I am aware it will be bad," said Crazy Horse. "And I cannot ask any man to expose his wife and children to the guns of the Bluecoats. I myself will never go in, but some of you have more to lose than I. It is for each man to decide for himself."

So it was that Black Elk and He Dog and their people started back for the agency, some trying not to look ashamed, some sorrowful at leaving the others to what seemed like certain death, and some hoping that perhaps at the agency they could get the guns and ammunition with which to make a stand later on. Nobody had any real hope, but some people tried to make it look that way.

As they were about to leave, it came to me that this would be the best time for me to go and see Lashuka. To get to the agency they had to cross the Powder River, where Two Moon's camp was, and I could go with them that far, see Lashuka, and return to Crazy Horse before any action began. I went to him and explained my idea, telling him it would be for only a short while. He looked at me for a few moments before speaking, and I saw how thin his face had become, making the scar beside his nose show up more clearly than ever. He must have been thinking of his own experience, when he lost the woman he loved to No Water, and was disgraced and almost killed when he tried to take her away. Finally he said, "This woman means a lot to you?"

"Yes," I replied.

"How is it you stay so long away from her?"

"I had to prove myself." I couldn't bring myself to say it was for her grandmother.

"Get back to her," he told me. "Or someone else will prove himself first."

That was what I was afraid of, so I thanked him and said I would return before the new grass came.

"Don't return unless you bring her with you," said Crazy Horse. "You'll be no good to me alone."

I promised, not knowing how soon, or in what unhappy state, I would bring her back.

Two Moon's camp consisted of forty lodges, on the west

side of the Powder River. The first person I saw, among those who came out to meet us, was Lone Wolf, and we greeted each other warmly. He had grown taller and stronger since I last saw him on my ill-fated eagle hunt, and I hoped I seemed bigger to him. I was worried about the sight I would present to Lashuka and, more important, to her grandmother. Before I could ask the question, he said, "You come at a good time."

"Why?" I asked, wondering if her grandmother had died.

"The old lady has demanded forty ponies, and Running Deer has only thirty. He's out right now, trying to steal the other ten."

"*Forty* ponies!" I had, all told, but six, and only one was fit for war.

"Forty," he repeated. "She's nearly blind, and wants to get the most she can while she still can count."

My mouth fell open and I put my hand in front of it quickly, to keep my soul from escaping. "Uh," I said. "What makes it a good time for me?"

"It's probably your last chance. If he comes back with the extra ten, the old lady will give Lashuka to him."

"I have to see her. Where is she?"

"The old lady?"

"No! Lashuka!"

He pointed out her lodge, and wished me luck. I walked slowly, wondering what there was to do. I'd have to think of something better than ponies to offer, but what? I had nothing to give but a love so strong it almost made me ill, and to her grandmother that counted less than bird tracks in wet snow. I decided I could only wait and see, and try to think of something on the spot. I paused beside the flap, then pulled it back and looked inside. At first all I could see was smoldering darkness, and I smelled the rancid smells of sickness and old age.

"Who's that?" came the croaking voice.

I decided to see how nearly blind she was, and said, "Lone Wolf."

"You don't sound like him."

"I have a message for Lashuka from Running Deer. Where is she?"

"What's the message? I'll give it to her."

"He asked that I give it to her alone."

"I said what's the message!"

I paused, and swallowed. "He says he hasn't been able to find any more ponies, so will go up into Crow country. He may be away a long while."

She digested this. "He must be crazy," she said, at last.

"That was his message. That's all I know." By now, my eyes could see into the darkness of the lodge, and I could see Lashuka wasn't there. "He asked that I tell her in person," I said.

"You still don't sound like Lone Wolf," said the old lady.

I coughed. "I may have caught the white man's sickness," I said. "It makes my voice sound different." I coughed again.

"She's down at the river, washing."

"Thank you." And, lying, I added, "May the Great Spirit heal your eyes."

"Too late for that," she croaked. "All I have left is my brain, and that's all I need."

You're right there, old lady, I said to myself. And there's nothing the matter with your brain. I let the flap fall back and turned toward the river, wondering how much time I had before Running Deer returned and revealed my lies. I reasoned that any time was better than none, and I must make the most of every moment.

I met her as she was coming back from the river, and my insides turned over at the sight of her face. She looked at me, wide-eyed, and almost dropped the washing, and then her whole face glowed. She didn't do anything because we were in public, but in a small voice she said, "You're back."

"That's right."

"You're well?"

"Yes."

"That's good." She started past me toward her lodge, not wanting to be seen talking.

"When can I see you?" I asked, hearing the echo of having said it before.

"I don't know. Where are you staying?"

I didn't know the answer, but I thought quickly and said, "Lone Wolf will know where I am. If he lets me, I'll stay with him."

She continued on, as though I hadn't spoken, and I watched her until she disappeared inside her lodge. I realized I was trembling and my knees felt watery, but I glowed in a way I can't describe—as though I'd caught the glow from Lashuka's face—and I wanted to shout "Yahoo!" like when I brought down my first buffalo. I jigged a little dance step, and went to look for Lone Wolf.

Lone Wolf had a tepee of his own, separate from his family's lodge, and he not only let me stay with him but also, with great tact, volunteered for night guard duty, so when Lashuka could get away she came to see me in his tepee. The main thing I remembered about those visits was the peace that came over me when she stepped inside, and the way the rest of the world dropped away into nothing. Everything important was in the twenty-foot circle enclosed by the lodge skins, and all the white men, pony soldiers, and even Running Deer were no more to me than mayflies in the spring. I told myself that if I were to die the next day I'd die happy, because there could be no greater happiness than what I had right now.

One night, as we were lying with our arms around each other, Lashuka said, "Do you ever think about the future?"

"All the time," I replied.

"What do you see?"

"You."

"Be serious. What's going to happen?"

"I don't care, so long as I have you."

"You know what I see? I see woods and brooks and rivers and a lake—a lake high in the mountains, with trees all around it, and water tinkling into it from one side and running out the other. I see it in my dreams sometimes—the most beautiful lake I've ever seen."

I sat up. "There's one like that in the *Paha Sapa*," I said. "I've seen it."

"I wonder why I should see it so often. It's got nothing to do with the future, but when I think about the future that's what I see."

I lay back again, and thought. "I guess it means the future is going to be good," I said, at last. "It was certainly a beautiful lake."

She turned her head toward me, and nuzzled my ear. "So are you," she said. "I think that'll be your new name—Chief Beautiful Lake. Would you like that?" I laughed, and she went on, "You say I'm your future, so that is your name."

My happiness was helped by the fact that Running Deer did not return; he was apparently having the kind of trouble I'd invented for him, and I wondered if he really would be so foolish as to go alone into Crow country, above the Yellowstone. I knew *I* would have, if I'd been doing it for Lashuka, but I also knew the odds against coming out alive were very poor. I was sure he wouldn't go that far.

One day, some Oglalas led by Last Bull came north from the Red Cloud agency, and they brought a grim story of misery and starvation through the winter. They had left the agency, they said, because anything was better than trying to live on the rotten rations, and they hoped to be able to do a little hunting before the soldiers brought them back. They knew they were making themselves into "hostiles," but they

126

said they'd rather be hostile and eat than be so-called good Indians and starve. It was an unhappy thought for Black Elk and He Dog and their people who were headed for the agency, and it kept them around Two Moon's camp a little while longer—long enough to see how wrong they'd been in thinking of going at all.

Running Deer returned early in March, the Moon-of-Snowblindness, bringing with him only three hungry ponies. He was in a bad humor, which was not made better by seeing me there, but it happened there were other things that took his mind off me. Rumors had been creeping around, like foxes in the night, of soldiers coming into our area. Some people believed them and some didn't; the treaty allowed us to hunt so long as we made war on nobody, and we were going out of our way to be peaceful, so who would bother us? True, we were supposed to go back to the agency, but few people thought the soldiers would be coming after us this soon. Old Bear and some of the other Big Bellies held the thought that the only reason the white men wanted us was to sell us their whisky and provisions, and the farther away we stayed from the whisky the better it would be for all concerned.

Then, one night, two young men, Wooden Leg and his brother, Yellow Hair, were out scouting and discovered a whole group of pony soldiers in a canyon east of the Powder River. They rode hurriedly into camp, making the wolf-howl and swinging their heads from side to side, which meant they had important news, and, when the council heard them, it was decided to move camp immediately. Heralds went about, calling out the word; the women took down the lodges and packed the provisions, and in a short time we were on our way down-river, away from the soldiers. We went to a spot just above where the Little Powder River flows into the Powder, in a canyon that gave us, we thought, good protection from attack. Our hunters and scouts watched the pony soldiers as they went over the hills westward, toward the Tongue River, and it seemed they hadn't been coming for us after all. Then winter, which had gone away for a short while, came back in full force with snow and freezing winds, and we felt safe. I now think, on looking back, that it's when you feel safe that you're in the greatest danger.

One day, a party was out hunting antelope along Otter Creek, just to the west of us, and spotted a whole camp full of pony soldiers. There were three troops of them, divided, as the soldiers always did, by the color of the horses: one troop of white horses, one of bay, and so on. The hunters turned and raced back toward camp, whipping their ponies, and those whose ponies gave out staggered on afoot, scrambling as fast as they could to bring the news. The canyon rang with their wolf calls as they came tumbling in, and in the general excitement a council of the Big Bellies was called. It was decided we were in the best place we could possibly be; we would send out a scouting party of ten men to keep watch on the soldiers, and post extra sentries around the camp that night. With these safeguards, and the walls of the canyon to protect us, we would have nothing to fear.

Running Deer was one of the ten scouts, and Lone Wolf and I were among those put on sentry duty. I was disappointed, because the scouts had the more important job, but at times like this you don't argue over an assignment. Running Deer was a member of the Crazy Dog *akicita*, and I, again, was only a guest.

It was cold that night, so cold that your nose burned when you breathed, and your breath hung in a white cloud in front of your face. Lone Wolf and I had the duty from the deepest part of the night until daylight, and when we went to our post, we saw that the men we were to relieve had built a fire and were huddled around its embers. I didn't think this was the best way to stand a watch, but I was in no position to criticize so I simply said, "Have you seen anything?"

Flat Fox, one of the two, looked at me sourly from the depths of his blanket, which he had wrapped around his head. "You don't look, you listen," he said. "If the scouts see anything, they'll send out a signal. Just keep your ears open."

Around-the-Bend, his partner, had been in a squatting position so long he seemed frozen there, and Flat Fox had to help him straighten up. "I hope the soldiers either attack us or drop out of sight," Around-the-Bend said, rubbing his arms and legs to bring back the blood. "One more night like this, and I'll walk with a crouch the rest of my life."

They tottered off toward camp, and Lone Wolf and I put more wood on the fire. It blazed brightly, sending sparks into the air, and while I knew this would make it harder to see in the darkness, I also knew we needed the heat. What we did was walk away from the fire on opposite sides, peer into the night until the cold began to numb our flesh, then walk back to the fire again. It was a good system, and would have been even better if we'd kept it up. After what seemed like half the night Lone Wolf said, "I have a thought. We don't get warm enough if we sit just a short while by the fire, so why not have one person walk while the other sits? There's no reason for us both to be cold at the same time."

This made sense, so I walked while he sat, and then he walked while I sat, and it did seem to work better. We fed the fire now and then, and all the time we listened for any signal from the scouts. Finally, when it had been my turn to sit by the fire, I closed my eyes a little, and when I opened them I saw Lone Wolf sitting across from me, with his eyes closed. I thought this strange, and decided it must be my turn to walk. I closed my eyes just once more, to gather the strength to stand up, and when I opened my eyes again the sky was pink, and the snowy tops of the hills around were light blue. Our fire was just a heap of blackened ash, and when I tried to stand my knees refused to move.

I rolled over onto all fours, and painfully began to straighten out. As I did I saw an old man trudging up the hill from camp, apparently to make his prayer to the rising sun. Some of the older people did this every day, but lately the bad weather had kept them in their lodges until the sun was well above the hills. I watched this old man as he reached the top of the ridge, and then I saw him stiffen, point his hand, and shout:

"The soldiers are right here! The soldiers are right here!"

I lurched to my feet and called to Lone Wolf, who thrashed around in his blanket and fell as he tried to rise. At that moment the first troop of soldiers, on white horses, charged into our camp, shooting their guns in all directions. The bullets zipped through the lodges, and suddenly there was mass panic. Women screamed, children ran about crying for their mothers, old people scrambled off trying to escape up the sides of the canyon, and the warriors, some of them naked out of their sleeping robes, groped for their weapons and tried to hold off the soldiers until the women and children could get away. Then, from the other side of camp, came a troop of soldiers on bay horses, and wherever you looked there were mounted Bluecoats, shooting at everything that moved. The shots and the screams and the shouting made the canyon ring, and the confusion was like a terrible dream.

My first thought was to get Lashuka to safety, and I raced to her tepee and found her just coming out, her hair all scrambled and her eyes wide with fear. She looked wildly about, and then saw me.

"Come on!" I shouted, taking her arm. "Come with me!"

"Help me with Grandmother!" she replied. "I can't move her!"

At that moment a Bluecoat on a bay horse came charging at us, aiming his gun. I still had my rifle from sentry duty, and I fired it at him blindly and he veered off. But he circled back at us again, and I grabbed Lashuka hard and pulled her off her feet. "Come on!" I said. "We'll get your grandmother later!" The trooper was coming at us again and we ran, bumping into other people who were running in all directions, and then I heard a gun go off close by, and didn't wait to see what happened. I reasoned that if I could get Lashuka to safety, there would be plenty of time to come back and fight. We headed toward the pony corral, but then I saw that a third troop of Bluecoats had got between us and our ponies, and were herding them away. Only a few strays were left out of more than twelve hundred horses, and they were running about in a dazed and frightened sort of way. I caught one by the mane, swung myself onto his back, then brought him around so Lashuka could climb on. She jumped up, nimble as an antelope, and put her arms around my waist.

"Maybe if we just ride past her tepee . . ." she started, but didn't finish the sentence. There were four or five troopers for every Indian warrior, and everywhere you looked there were men in blue, shooting, shouting, and slashing.

"I'd like to, but I can't," I said. "We'll be lucky if we can get away ourselves."

"All right," she said. "But let's come back when it's all over."

This was such a wild idea that I didn't even bother to reply. Nobody could tell what would be happening when it was over; we might all be dead or scattered to the four great directions, and to think of coming back was, at this point, just trying to rub out the guilty feeling of leaving the old lady behind. It was better than cutting out without even a thought, but it certainly didn't deserve an answer.

As we went toward the higher land I saw women and

children and old people trudging upward through the snow, some carrying packs and some trying to carry each other, and their wails and shrieks were louder here than the sounds of battle. They were like little grubs leaving a burning log, traveling blindly and painfully just to be anywhere except in the fire. I saw one woman who had a pack on her back, a child under one arm, and another child holding her free hand; they were all weeping, and the woman was about to fall down from exhaustion. I put the older child in front of me on the pony, and Lashuka took the baby, and slowly we made our way up to the rim of the canyon. Then I let them off, and went back to rejoin the fight.

By the time I got there, it was almost over; there were just too many Bluecoats. I saw Two Moon, Bear-Walks-on-a-Ridge, and Wooden Leg hiding behind a rock, while Two Moon made medicine over his repeating rifle to make sure it shot well. He stood it on end in front of him and passed his hands up and down the barrel without touching it, all the time muttering his chant, and then he pointed to a nearby trooper and said, "My medicine is good; watch me kill that soldier." He raised his gun, aimed, and fired. He missed. Then Bear-Walks-on-a-Ridge, who had an old muzzle-loading rifle, took aim and fired, and the trooper lurched and fell forward, a bullet in the back of his head. The three rushed out and stabbed and beat him to death, and I ran to help them. Wooden Leg stripped off the trooper's blue coat, and the others searched his body for whatever they wanted, and I picked up his rifle, which had dropped to one side as he fell. It was a Winchester repeater, one of the best, and I felt very lucky.

But few of us had guns; most had bows and arrows, and they weren't enough. The troopers beat us out of camp, and we retreated up the side of the canyon and watched while they burned our lodges and everything in them—everything except what they took for themselves. All our *wasna*, our dried meat, and our clothes were gone, as well as the ammunition that popped and flared in the smoky fires. We were left with what clothes we had on, the few ponies we'd managed to save, and no food except some bits of dried meat the women had snatched as they made their packs. On the bright side, we lost only one man killed and one badly wounded—I guess in a fight as confused as that nobody can shoot straight —while the Bluecoats lost several. The badly wounded man had his forearm shattered by a bullet; Braided Locks, who was luckier, had a bullet crease the skin of one cheek without hitting bone.

As we gathered with the women and children and old people at the rim of the canyon, we tried to sort out what had happened, and how the Bluecoats had got past our scouts as well as our line of sentries.

Running Deer and the other scouts were forced to admit that they missed the troopers in the stormy darkness, and came across their trail only after the troopers had gone past. Running Deer gave a stirring description of how they lashed their ponies to get back to warn us, and how the ponies had one by one become winded, and they hadn't reached camp until the battle was already on. His report was received in silence. Then the sentries were questioned, and I, truthfully, said I had heard and seen nothing until I saw the old man give the alarm. I asked myself in my heart if it would do any good to admit I'd been asleep, and I reasoned it would do nothing but harm, because even if I'd been wide awake and pacing my beat I might not have seen the soldiers before the old man did. Lone Wolf apparently felt the same way, because he gave the same report I did. It was concluded that the night and the bad weather had beaten us, and no more was said about it.

We who had saved horses stayed behind to guard the rear, while the ragged column of survivors waded the icy Powder River and set off to the east. When we stopped for the night, a count showed that aside from the one warrior who'd been killed, only one person was missing: Lashuka's grandmother. Lashuka looked at me in silence, and then said, "I'm going back for her."

"Don't be foolish," I replied.

"I said I was going back, and I am."

"Listen to me," I said. "You can't tell what's down there now. It would be dangerous, and beyond that pointless. What can you gain?"

"If she's alive I'll bring her back. If she isn't, I'll bury her."

Clearly, this was nothing for Lashuka to be doing, so I said, "You stay here. I'll take a party back, and look for her."

"You don't have to. This is my affair."

"Yes, I do have to. Now, stay here and stop worrying." I spoke to her almost as though we were married, and she obeyed me the same way. To be honest about it, it gave me a small feeling of pleasure.

I got some others who had horses, and asked them to come back with me to the camp. I cannot say I hoped the old lady was dead, which seemed likely, but I must admit I looked forward to the idea of being able to see Lashuka without her. What I wanted was just to ride away and pretend she never existed.

We could smell the ruins of the camp long before we reached it. The burning buffalo hides of the tepees gave off a bitter, oily smell, and this mixed with the smoke from burning clothing and blankets and hair filled the night with a stench that almost made us sick. Every camp or village has its smells—the smell of people and cooking and waste matter and the rest—and these are good, and comforting, but when they are reduced to ash there comes a sour and rancid smell in the air, that reeks of misery and despair. It is a hollow, cold smell, and it chills your bones.

As we picked our way down the side of the canyon we could see, amid the smoking rubble, that one tepee was still left standing. It was roughly where Lashuka's lodge had been, and as we approached I realized it was hers. Hardly daring to look, I pulled aside the flap and there, in the darkness, I could just make out the figure of the old woman, lying in her sleeping robe. I thought she must be dead, because the lodge was full of bullet holes. I was about to suggest we leave her there when she spoke, and her cackling voice made us all jump.

"Who's there?" she said.

"Dark Elk," I replied, forgetting she didn't know I was around.

"You." Her voice was rich with contempt. "What are you doing here?"

"We came back to get you."

"You don't sound happy about it," she said.

"It's been a long day," I replied, which didn't answer her implied question.

"You know," said Lone Wolf, who was beside me, "those troopers must have good hearts, after all."

"Why?" said Spotted Crow, looking around at the wreckage.

"They didn't kill the old lady."

"It's not because they didn't try," she said, sitting up. "The bullets were buzzing through here like bees. Where's Lashuka?"

"With the others," I replied.

She pulled herself to her feet. "Take me to her."

I said nothing and reached for her arm.

"I have an idea," said Spotted Crow. "I think the troopers can't be far from here."

"Why?" asked Lone Wolf.

"You don't go any farther than you have to, after a battle. They know we're going away, and I think they made camp early. Besides, they have some wounded. They'll want to stop."

We all looked at him, to see what he had in mind.

"I think we should go look for them, and try to get our ponies back."

We considered this in silence. There were only twelve of us, and several hundred soldiers. Still, our need for horses was great enough to make it worth trying.

"All right," I said. "Let's do it."

"Not you," the old lady put in. "You're taking me to Lashuka."

I ground my teeth. "Later," I said.

"Now." Her claw-like hand tightened on my forearm. "Put me on your pony."

Trying not to sigh out loud I mounted, and the others helped her up behind me. Her talons dug into my sides. "Good luck," I said to Spotted Crow, and headed slowly up the canyon trail.

I heard them ride off in the darkness, and I ached to be with them. I wondered if I could deliver the old lady and then catch up with them, but serious thought told me this was impossible. Behind me, she kept up a running stream of comment and complaint.

"Who made Lashuka go off and leave me?" she asked. "Was it you?"

"It was a trooper," I replied. "On a bay horse."

"I heard her ask someone to help her with me. Was that you?"

"Yes."

"I might have known. You ran."

"I told you, it was the trooper. He was shooting at us."

"That doesn't make you different. They were shooting at everybody."

I took a deep breath, and tried to be calm. "This one trooper," I said, "came straight at Lashuka and me. The only thing we could do was run."

"You could have shot him."

"I did, but I missed."

"He couldn't have been very close."

I bit my lips. "Old lady," I said, "with all respect, I would like to point out that in a battle things don't always work out the way they should. You can be standing right next to a man, and still not hit him."

"Don't tell me about battles. I've been through more battles than you'll see if you live to be a hundred. When I was a girl there wasn't a moon passed but we had three or four good battles, some against the Crows and Pawnees, and some against the Bluecoats. Try to tell me about battles, and I'll tell you things that'll make the hair fly off your head."

"Did you fight in them?" I asked, gently, thinking to score a point.

"As good as. We girls and women would stand on a hill nearby and do the trilling to make the warriors' hearts good, and sometimes we'd rush in and stampede the enemy horses. Shouting, waving blankets—many's the pony herd we drove off while the men were fighting on foot. Then after the battle we'd run in and cut up the enemy dead—those who'd lost husbands or sons would do it for revenge, and the rest of us did it for the spirit of the thing. Sometimes we'd cut off the

139

arms and legs, and sometimes just cut off the—well, never mind. I don't need *you* to tell me about battles."

"I guess not," I said.

There was a short silence, then she said, "Where have you been?"

"I told you. I took Lashuka to join the others."

"I mean since I last saw you. Last thing I knew, you had the nerve to try to come courting, with no more than one pony to your name. Where have you been since then?"

"Many places. Mostly with Crazy Horse." I thought this might impress her.

"How many ponies do you have now?"

I paused. "I had many," I replied, being evasive about the number. "But the Bluecoats drove them off this morning. Now all I have is this one, and he doesn't belong to me."

She cackled. "You'll never get Lashuka that way."

"I imagine Running Deer's ponies were driven off, too," I said, with satisfaction. "He probably has no more than I do, right now."

She considered this, then said, "I've heard your voice in the last little while. Where?"

"I have no idea."

"I do. Were you the one who came around saying you were Lone Wolf, and had a message from Running Deer?"

"Me?" I said, trying to think of an answer.

"I'm not talking to the pony."

"Why would I do that?"

"Why do you do anything? Why did you take Lashuka from me this morning, except to hope I'd be killed?"

140

"I've already told you. The trooper drove us off."

"I heard you. It's a thin story."

There was nothing I could say, so I remained silent. After what seemed like a long time we reached the spot where the others had bedded down for the night, and I delivered the old lady to her granddaughter. Lashuka was so grateful her eyes filled with tears—or maybe she was just glad to see the old wolf, I don't know which.

"Grandmother!" she exclaimed. "You're alive!"

"No thanks to him," her grandmother replied, sliding to the ground.

"We tried not to leave you, but the troopers chased us off."

Her grandmother sniffed, and said, "So he tried to tell me. What's in the pot? I haven't eaten all day."

"There's almost no food. Very few people saved anything."

"If you had any decent hunters, they'd have shot something. What have you been doing all day, except running away?"

Lashuka led her off, looking back over her shoulder at me with a glance that spoke thanks and compassion and—I liked to believe—love, and I went off to find a place to lie down. As they moved into the darkness I heard the old lady saying ". . . rudest young man I've ever seen. Leaves me to the soldiers hoping I'll be killed, then comes back and has the gall to try and tell me about battles. When I was his age I'd been in more battles than . . ." I wrapped my blanket around my head, and lay down to sleep. It had, as I told the old lady earlier, been a long day.

Shortly after sunrise we heard the rumble of many hooves, and in a while Lone Wolf, Spotted Crow, and the others rode up laughing, as they herded a whole mass of our ponies they'd been able to take away from the sleeping Bluecoats. They could have taken more, they said, but they reasoned it was best to take only as many as they could manage. Besides, the soldiers had finally awakened and shot at them, so they decided not to get into a battle. I felt real misery that I hadn't been with them, because they were heroes at a time when we needed heroes badly. I, as usual, had been doing something else while heroic deeds were being done by others.

Those of us who had come from the Crazy Horse camp remembered the way back, and we led the sad procession eastward and northward, hoping once and for all to get clear of the Bluecoats. We found out, much later, that the raid had been led by a Bird Chief named Reynolds, and that his chief, Three Stars Crook, had been so angry at him for letting us escape and get back some of our ponies that he'd called a council of other chiefs to punish Reynolds. This, we thought, was a good joke on Reynolds, but it came a little late.

9

We spent three nights on the march. The earth froze hard at night and it was bitter cold, and although only a few had blankets or robes there was no sickness—why, I cannot imagine. In the daytime the earth thawed a little, and there was mud and icy water, and those who couldn't ride were forced to slog along on feet that became wet and cold and numb no matter how heavily they were wrapped. Again for no reason I can think of, nobody suffered frozen toes, or any of the other griefs that usually come with such conditions. We had little to eat, and all in all it was the most unpleasant three days I can remember. If we hadn't known where we were going, I think a lot of us might have given up. There are many people, especially among the older ones, who are able to lie right down and die, when they want to. I have seen it done.

I, on the other hand, had everything to live for. Lashuka was with us, and although she was escorted by her grandmother and attended by Running Deer, the mere knowledge that she and I were going in the same direction was enough to keep me happy. Running Deer felt, and probably rightly, that he'd lost face when he and the other scouts let the Bluecoats get past them, and he was doing everything he could to make up to Lashuka. Of course the harder he tried, the sillier he made himself look, and as I saw it, I had nothing to worry about. At one point I rode close enough to hear him saying " . . . if it hadn't been for the snow. Not a weasel could have escaped us that night, and we were done in by a freak blizzard. I've heard the white men can make it snow when they want, and I'm sure they did just that, that night. It was worse than any natural snow I've ever . . ." I rode away, smiling to myself. Lashuka, I felt sure, was doing the same thing.

We reached Crazy Horse's camp on the fourth day, and the Oglalas gave us food and blankets and clothing. From all sides you could hear people saying, "Cheyennes, come and eat here," and when we had eaten they arranged for us to stay among them in their lodges, until we could find shelter of our own. Laughing Hawk took Lone Wolf and me into his tepee, and to me it was like staying with two brothers. They had both been good to me, and now in thanks I gave Laughing Hawk my new rifle, the one I took from the trooper. He didn't want to take it but I insisted, so in return he gave me a bow and a quiver full of arrows, since mine had been destroyed by the Bluecoats. I still had my old rifle and four shells, so I was better off than many. Then Laughing Hawk gave his old rifle to Lone Wolf, and we all had fighting equipment of a sort.

The chiefs gathered in the council lodge that night, and Crazy Horse was glad to see that the raid had wiped forever from the minds of He Dog and Black Elk the idea of going to the agency. They had once been willing to submit, but now it was as though the agency had never been, and their only thought was to fight the Bluecoats on better terms than before. Two Moon, who had tried his best to avoid the soldiers, had seen his camp wiped out, his horses stolen, and one of his people killed, and he was now ready to fight. This was good news to Crazy Horse, because if the raid had not come when it did, all these people would have gone to the agency, and been lost to us as warriors.

It was decided to move to the northeast, to the mouth of the Tongue River, where there was a large camp of Hunkpapa Sioux. Their chief and powerful medicine man was Buffalo-Bull-Sitting-Down, known as Sitting Bull for short, and if we joined with them we would have a good fighting group. Sitting Bull was one of those who wanted nothing to do with the white men, but if forced into a fight he would make it hard on whoever attacked him. Many of the smaller groups of Lakota liked to stay near the Hunkpapa camp, in case of trouble. Sitting Bull was like a father to all free Lakotas.

So, next morning, the herald went riding through the camp, making the usual announcements that go with moving, and before the sun was overhead the lodges were down, the travois packed, and we were on our way. The Oglalas loaned ponies to all Cheyennes who had none, so nobody had to walk. The women and children were, as always, near the rear of the long column, and Running Deer kept riding back to make sure all was well with Lashuka and her grandmother. I figured he must have exhausted his excuses by this time, and had turned back to the more serious business of courting, but I felt I was in no danger. I bided my time, gathering great security in the memory of the nights in Lone Wolf's tepee. It is a good thing to have that kind of memory, because it almost keeps you from being jealous.

We were three days getting to the Hunkpapa camp, and when we arrived the welcome was like that the Oglalas gave the Cheyennes, only more so. As soon as we came in sight the Hunkpapa women put their kettles on the fire, and two big special lodges were set up in the camp circle, one for our men and one for our women. We went into these, and then girls appeared in pairs, carrying steaming kettles of meat

146

between them, and they kept coming with the meat until we'd eaten our fill, and had enough left over for the next day. I couldn't remember when I'd eaten so much, or been so bloated afterward. That was the way we lived—eat as much as you can while you can, and make the memory of it last when you're hungry.

Next a Hunkpapa herald rode about, calling out: "The soldiers have made the Cheyennes very poor! Very poor! All who have blankets or robes or tepees to spare should give them! O, the soldiers have made the Cheyennes very poor!" As I said before, heralds love to hear themselves talk, but in this case it was a welcome sound. People came crowding around us with gifts. Men, women, and children gave us blankets, clothes, tepees, horses, robes—anything we needed to set up a camp like ours was before the soldiers wiped us out. A ten-year-old girl put a buffalo robe in front of Wooden Leg, and left it there because she was too shy to put it into his hands. A Hunkpapa man gave Wooden Leg's father a medicine pipe, to replace the one that had been lost. In short, anyone who needed anything got it immediately and without question, until you were almost embarrassed to accept anything more. I, who had lost little, took only the few things I needed, but others got quite a lot. Lashuka and her grandmother got a small tepee, clothes, and cooking utensils.

(I suppose I should explain here that Wooden Leg got his name not because he had one—we didn't use that sort of thing—but because when he was young he was able to walk farther and for a longer time than anyone else, and people said his legs must be made of wood not to get tired. Strangely, he wasn't a very good runner.)

There was some ammunition, too, although not much. It was hard for us to get ammunition because the Government naturally wouldn't let us have it if they could help it; they only gave it to the "friendlies" to use for hunting. The Gros Ventres were among these so-called friendly tribes, and they'd come to Sitting Bull's camp, traded off all their arms and powder, and then returned to their agency and said the Lakotas had stolen it from them. That way they got a new issue, and everyone was happy. But still, we didn't have enough for a long war with the soldiers.

Nobody wanted this war except some of the younger warriors; we had joined Sitting Bull because of the strength it would give us if we were attacked, and because of his desire to keep away from the whites. He told those who wanted war it was foolish because it wasted energy, and that energy ought to be put to use getting food and clothing for our families. But I think everyone knew we'd have to fight sooner or later, and all we could do was make ourselves as strong as possible. That was why the Oglalas, in a special council, decided they should have one leader only, a man who could lead the warriors and at the same time be a good father to his people. These duties had been divided between the Big Bellies and the warriors' societies, but often bickering and jealousy got in the way, and the result was either action of a useless sort or no action at all. The Oglalas decided they could no longer afford this luxury, and there was

148

only one man who could bring them all together. That man, naturally, was Crazy Horse. His vision of leading his people was fulfilled.

Some Minneconjoux Lakotas led by Lame Deer had joined the Hunkpapa camp shortly after we arrived, and when word of Crazy Horse's new position spread through the hills more and more people came flocking in. Our camp consisted of four bands: the Hunkpapas, the Oglalas, the Minneconjoux, and the Cheyennes, in that order of size, and as more groups joined, it became necessary to keep moving, to find food. Our scouts reported buffalo up in the Rosebud country to the north, so we went northward by slow stages, and were joined along the way by the Arrows-All-Gone Lakotas (known also as the Sans Arcs, or No Bows), the Blackfoot Lakotas, and a few Santees, who were called the Waist and Skirt, or No-Clothing People. They were so poor they had dogs instead of horses to pull their travois, and their women made dresses in two pieces instead of one, which was the usual way. There was also a sprinkling of Assiniboines and Brulé Lakotas, and, at the Powder River, we were joined by Chief Lame White Man and a big band of Cheyennes. By now a lot of "friendlies" were coming in, some because of conditions at the agencies and some who'd heard of Reynolds' attack on our camp, and of all of them the biggest surprise was Red Cloud's eighteen-year-old son, Jack, bringing with him the silver-inlaid rifle the white men had given his father in Washington. We went westward from the Powder to the Tongue, where we met with another band of

Cheyennes under Dirty Moccasins, and they brought with them extra ammunition, sugar, coffee, and tobacco, and by their number made the Cheyenne circle of lodges twice what it had been when we went to Sitting Bull. The Lakotas had grown in number, too, until it was estimated that Crazy Horse had three thousand warriors under his command. By now I was spending more time with the Cheyennes than with the Oglalas, trying to see as much of Lashuka as I could. This wasn't easy, because of her grandmother, and because Running Deer was always snooping around. But one evening I saw her go down to the river for water, and I snatched a fishing line and followed as fast as I could. I threw the un-baited hook in the stream, and as Lashuka was filling her jars I moved toward her. She saw me, but pretended not to.

"How are you?" I asked.

"Well." Still not looking at me.

"Can I see you tonight?"

"I can't get out."

"Why not?"

"Grandmother sleeps across the entrance. I'd have to step on her to leave."

"Doesn't she trust you?"

"No."

I thought for a moment, then said, "I'll come to the op-posite side. Loosen the skins a little at the bottom."

She said nothing as she slung her jars around her neck and started back, so I assumed she agreed. That night, when the camp was dark, I went to her tepee and knelt down at the west side, opposite the entrance, and tugged gently at the covering. It was loose, so I rolled it up a bit, lay on my stomach, and forced my head and arms through into the tepee. Lashuka was just on the other side, and beyond her I could hear her grandmother snoring.

"Come on out," I whispered.

"No," she said, and got down and rubbed her face against mine. The smell of her, as always, made me slightly dizzy.

"Why not?" I said. "You can come back the same way."

"If she found out, I'd never get out again. She's suspicious, because she knows I like you better than Running Deer."

This made me feel warm inside, and I decided if she didn't want to come out she didn't have to. I was content to stay right where I was, rubbing my face against hers and making small and meaningless noises. I say "meaningless" in that they weren't words; they meant a great deal, but there was nothing that could be done about it at the time. I was almost unconscious with pleasure when I felt a slash like fire across my legs, and then another, and someone outside was shouting. I scrambled backward and into Running Deer, who was cutting at my behind with his pony whip and crying "Thief! Plunderer! Sneak!"

"Stop it!" I shouted, grabbing his arms. "It's Dark Elk! Stop it!"

By now several people were awake and coming toward us, and Running Deer pretended he hadn't known who I was. "I'm sorry," he said. "I thought someone was trying to sneak into the lodge."

"I was talking with Lashuka," I replied, hearing her grand-mother's voice and wanting to get away as fast as I could.

"You chose a funny way to do it," said Running Deer, with a smirk. "I prefer to talk to her the approved way, standing up."

"Impossible," I said, and turned and walked quickly away. Behind me, I could hear Lashuka's grandmother coming out of the lodge, loudly demanding to know what was going on. I felt that perhaps my time in the Cheyenne camp had come to an end for a while.

The problem was that if there should be a battle, I honestly didn't know where I would go. Crazy Horse was the best leader, but I felt if I fought with the Cheyennes and fought well, Lashuka and her grandmother would be more likely to hear of it. Also, Crazy Horse's idea of fighting as a group, rather than singly, cut down on the chances of doing any great deeds alone. It was an odd problem, and I decided to let time and conditions solve it for me. If I'd learned anything, it was that you can't tell in advance what's going to happen in a battle. If you know what's going on during the battle itself, you can count yourself lucky.

It was the middle of May, the Moon-of-Shedding-Ponies, when we reached the Rosebud, a few miles upstream from the Elk, or Yellowstone, River. We made six great camp circles, which stretched out along the valley, and with the lodges and our pony herds it was impossible to see from one end of the encampment to the other. We moved every few days, while the hunters went out for buffalo and the ponies filled themselves with new grass. In all we moved five times, a few miles at a time, and each time the Cheyenne circle was at the front of the encampment, and the Hunkpapas at the rear. The Oglalas were about in the middle.

It was at this last camp that I heard the Hunkpapas were going to hold a medicine dance, sometimes called a sun dance, and it came to me that this would be a good time for me to join in, and test my endurance. It was now early June, the Moon-of-Making-Fat, and the sun was highest and the growing power of the world the strongest. There is a great deal of ceremony connected with a sun dance; a sacred tree is cut down, trimmed, and planted in the middle of the dance circle, and then the dancers, who've been fasting and purifying themselves, have slits cut in the skin of their back or chest, and rawhide thongs are passed through and tied, the other end being tied to the top of the tree. They then dance around, straining against the thongs, until they either faint or the rawhide tears loose from their flesh. There is also a lot of feasting and praying and chanting, and children are given free rein to do pretty much as they please. Their game is to torture any passing adult, because during the three days of the dance nobody is supposed to show any reaction to pain. It is, as I said, a generally purifying and strengthening experience.

Word passed through the camps about the dance of the Hunkpapas, which was being held up near the Deer Medicine rocks. These are towers of rock, thought to be sacred, and in the old days Cheyenne and Lakota hunters would go there and pray, before setting out after antelope or deer. Sitting Bull, who as chief medicine man was the leader of the dance, had prepared for it in an unusual way: he'd given one hundred pieces of his flesh, cut out of both forearms with an awl and snipped off, while he sang his medicine song. It promised to be a great dance, although at the time nobody could know how really memorable it would be. Historic is probably a better word.

I stripped down to my breechcloth and painted my body, then set out for the Deer Medicine rocks. Many others were going too, and as we neared the place it was so crowded you could hardly see the dancing ground. I pressed forward, and as I worked through the throng I felt a sharp stab of pain in my ribs. I clapped my hand to my side and turned, and was greeted by shrieks of laughter from a small boy, holding the piece of spear grass with which he'd just stabbed me. He darted away and I checked my instinct to chase him, remembering this was all a part of the sun dance. I rubbed my side, and my hand came away with a small smear of blood. I told myself to forget it; that this was just a prelude to the pain I was about to endure. For some reason the unexpected pain hurt more than I felt it should, and this irritated me.

But I never got to feel the real pain. As I got closer to the dance circle people were reluctant to let me through, because there was apparently something special going on. I could hear chanting and the beat of the drums, and see dust rising from the circle, but I couldn't see what was happening.

I tried to edge past one tall Minneconjou, whose chest was scarred from many dances, and he turned and looked at me coldly.

"What do you want?" he asked.

"Excuse me," I said. "I want to join the dance."

He regarded me with contempt. "You a Hunkpapa?"

"No, an Oglala. A Cheyenne, really. I came with Crazy Horse."

"This dance is for Hunkpapas only."

"Only?" I couldn't believe it, but he turned away and someone else nodded in agreement. So there it was. I was all painted and ready to prove my courage, and the only problem was I came from the wrong camp. To hide my disappointment I tried to pretend it didn't matter and that I'd really come to watch the dance, and I stood as tall as I could and peered over and around the heads in front of me. There were some people doing the regular dance with the thongs, but everybody's interest seemed to be on something else. I felt a touch on my arm, and looked around and saw my Oglala friend Laughing Hawk.

"Can you see anything?" he asked.

"Not much," I replied. "What's happening?"

"Sitting Bull. He's doing his dance."

"What's so unusual about it?"

"He's looking into the sun. He hasn't taken his eyes off the sun since he started."

I thought about this. "That ought to bring some sort of results," I said, at last. "Won't he go blind?"

Laughing Hawk shrugged. "Time will tell."

And time did tell, but it took all of that day, and night, and until about noon the following day. Sitting Bull kept dancing, always looking into the sun, and when the sun had set he kept right on dancing, working his way around so he was facing it when it rose the next morning. Laughing Hawk and I drifted away and made some plans for hunting, and then I went off to look for Lashuka. I couldn't find her, and assumed she was off on some errand for her grandmother. So I went back to my small tepee, which had been given me by the Hunkpapas, and went to sleep. Far away, I could still hear the drums of the medicine dance.

Next morning I went back, and found Sitting Bull still treading away, mumbling his chant. This time I was able to get close enough to the circle to see him, and it was an impressive sight. His arms were covered with dried blood, his eyes were red and appeared sightless, and his massive chest, almost as thick as a buffalo's, was wet with sweat. He glistened in the rays of the sun, and he seemed somehow to be drawing power from it. You could see why this was called a sun dance.

Then, when the sun was directly overhead and he had to lean back to look into it, his steps faltered; he staggered and almost went over backward, then caught himself while everyone held their breath. He was like a wounded warrior, trying to stay upright in a shower of arrows; then suddenly he collapsed and sank limply to the ground, his wide-open eyes still staring at the sun. Someone got a water skin and emptied

156

it on him, but he didn't move; the water appeared to steam as it touched him, and it sank quickly into the ground. People went down to the river in relays, bringing back water and throwing it on him, and this went on for a long time before his feet twitched, then his hands moved, and he blinked his eyes. Two warriors helped him up and took him into the medicine lodge, and for a long time there was silence. I wondered if it was possible he could have stared at the sun so long without being blinded, but I'd noticed as he was led away that although his eyes were red, he seemed able to see. He must have had very strong medicine.

There came a great commotion inside the lodge, with much noise of approval and rejoicing, and we all gathered around. Finally, the flap opened and one of the Hunkpapa Big Bellies came out, and told us that Sitting Bull had had a vision. He'd heard a chant from the sun, which went: "Now he is walking, now he is walking, this is a buffalo bull walking," and then a voice had called out: "I give you these because they have no ears," and he had looked up and seen many Bluecoats falling upside down into our camp. They had no ears, and their hats were falling off. This could mean only one thing: that soldiers were going to come to our camp, and because they were upside down it meant they would be killed. We all cheered and began chanting victory songs, and runners went out to pass the word.

By this time the ponies had cropped most of the grass and the game was thinning out, so the whole encampment moved over the hills to Ash Creek, which empties into the river we call the Greasy Grass and the whites call the Little Bighorn. We knew from Sitting Bull's vision that Bluecoats would come into camp, but we didn't know from where, so it was decided to send scouts out in all directions, to be safe. Long Hair Custer had been reported on the Powder River, but had turned north toward the Yellowstone, and was probably far away by now.

A few days later, when it was the Elk *akicita*'s turn to do scouting duty, Little Hawk, one of their leaders, formed a party. He chose White Bird and his cousin Yellow Eagle and then, although I was not a member, he saw me standing by and said, "Dark Elk, will you come with us?"

I was astounded, because this was almost like being invited to join the *akicita*, and for a moment I couldn't find words. Then I said, "I would be happy to," trying to sound as though it was something I did every day, and went to get my pony.

We rode southward over the hills, toward the Rosebud. Little Hawk glanced at my pony, whose best days had long since passed, and said, "It would be good if we could get some horses from the white people. I think we could use a few."

"I know I could," I said, knowing what he meant. "My best pony was lost in Reynolds' raid, and this was all I could find." I had a feeling we were out for something more important than a horse raid—and as it turned out I was right. But, just to go along with Little Hawk, I said, "My theory is a man can't have too many ponies."

Little Hawk laughed. "That's as true a statement as was ever made," he said.

We followed the Rosebud over rough terrain up to the head of the creek, then went back down the Tongue River to the north, and across to the Rosebud again. It was one of those clear days in spring, when the sky is bright and the wind gentle and warm, and we could smell the roses that bloomed by the thousands along the valley. When we reached the river we saw two other scouts, Crooked Nose and Little Shield, who was an Arapaho. They joined us, and we all made camp for the night. So far, our scouting had been nothing but a pleasant ride.

Next day, at the big bend in the Rosebud, we saw some buffalo bulls, and Little Hawk killed one. It wasn't very fat but we skinned it, and started a fire, and we were cutting the meat into strips when Yellow Eagle said, "Look! There's better meat there!" We looked, and saw a herd of cows running over the hills to the south, running fast as though they'd been frightened.

Little Hawk watched them for a moment, then said, "Come on. Crooked Nose, you stay here and roast this meat. We'll see if we can't get something a little fatter."

We mounted our ponies and set off toward the cows, and had covered maybe half the distance when I happened to look around. Crooked Nose was standing away from the fire and making frantic motions from side to side, which was the signal to come back. I told Little Hawk, and when he saw Crooked Nose's signals he turned his pony fast, and we all raced back to the fire. When we got there, Crooked Nose was excited. He pointed to a hill, where there were two red buttes outlined against the bright sky.

"I saw two men looking over there," he said. "They looked for a while, and then they rode up in plain sight. Each one was leading a horse. They went out of sight coming toward us—I think they're headed this way."

Little Hawk thought about this, then smiled. "They must be Lakotas," he said. "Let's have some fun with them. We'll give them a fright." We headed for where the men had last been seen. Little Hawk's idea was to ambush them and pretend to capture them, and we rode along a gulch to keep out of sight. Then, when we'd gone a short distance, he got off his pony and crept to the crest of the hill and looked over. I saw his eyes widen, and he sucked in his breath and ducked back quickly. "Soldiers!" he hissed. "The country is black with them!" He leaped on his pony, and we galloped back to the fire and stamped it out. He lost his field glasses in the rush, but there was no time to stop for them now. We hurried down to the river bank, where there were trees and bushes to hide us, and then we rode as hard as we could up toward the head of the stream, the bushes whipping our faces and tearing at our hair. We finally came out of the timber on a high butte about three miles away, and looked back on the black mass of soldiers marching toward the river. There were pony soldiers and walking soldiers and wagons and pack mules; it was a whole expedition, and if we hadn't stopped to cook the buffalo we would have ridden right into them. Crooked Nose and Little Shield split off to alert their village, and the rest of us headed through the foothills of the Wolf Mountains toward ours.

We reached camp just as day was breaking, and we gave the wolf howl and swung our heads from side to side. People came running out to meet us, and the sides of the council lodge were rolled up so all could hear what we had to report. When Little Hawk told of the soldiers a great roar went up, and everyone began to make ready for war. Scouts were sent out to look for the soldiers and report their movements, and they galloped away, shouting and whipping their ponies in their excitement. The rest of us went about the business of painting our bodies, sharpening our knives, and making whatever medicine we thought best for our own protection. In some cases older men instructed their sons in the medicine, showing them the proper procedure for such things as putting on the warbonnet. (You lift it from the ground, then face the sunrise singing, and three times bring the bonnet near your head, then on the fourth time put it on—all this, of course, if you've attained the maturity as a fighter to warrant wearing one.) There is also special medicine that people work on their ponies, some throwing badger dust on their hooves, others standing them in water for a certain time, and also tying up their tails with eagle feathers and painting them with colored medicine stripes. Some like to run their ponies back and forth or around in circles, so they'll get their second wind before the fighting starts. Everyone has his own system, and there have been times when the preparations for a battle took longer than the battle itself.

When we were ready, we rode four times around the

camp circle while the women made their trilling noise, and then, with Little Hawk in charge of one party and young Two Moon in charge of another, we rode back into the Wolf Mountains. I was with Little Hawk's group, and among the the two hundred or so with young Two Moon were a brother and sister, Chief Comes-in-Sight and Buffalo-Calf-Road-Woman. She prided herself on never having missed a battle, and this put me in mind of Lashuka's grandmother, and I vowed that on this day I'd do enough great deeds to make the old lady change her opinion of me. For some reason I wasn't nervous; the old dry-mouth feeling was gone and I seemed to be moving without effort or conscious thought, as though I were dreaming. Lone Wolf rode beside me as we went out, and his face was tense beneath his red-and-black war paint. I tried to cheer him, and said, "You know what the Lakotas say—'This is a good day to die. Only the earth and the sky last forever.'"

"Thank you," said Lone Wolf.

"Do you feel well?"

"No."

I didn't want to ask if he was afraid, so I said, "What kind of sickness is it?"

"It's my crazy brother," he replied. "He's not quite thirteen, and he wants to fight."

I remembered his brother as the little boy who was pestering us the day I first saw Lashuka, and I couldn't imagine his being a warrior. We'd called him Fat Bug. "What's his name now?" I asked.

"We still call him Fat Bug," Lone Wolf replied. "But he doesn't like it. He wants to be called Bear-That-Roars-Like-a-Bull."

"He'll have to do something to deserve that name," I said.

"I know. And I'm afraid he's going to try." Lone Wolf looked around at the rear of the column, as though expecting his brother to be coming after us. "I told him someone had to stay in camp to guard the weak ones, but he said that was a job for the Big Bellies and old people."

"Can't your father make him stay?"

"I hope so."

"Well, if I see him I'll tell him to go home."

Lone Wolf smiled thinly. "It will take more than that," he said. "You'll have to tie him to a tree if you want to stop him."

"Then I'll do that." It made me feel good to think there was someone younger and less experienced than I, and it gave me a confidence in myself that made everything all right.

We rode for most of the night, and when we could smell the river we stopped, and rested our horses. Little Hawk had directed that everyone hold back, so as not to have wild young men go rushing out and alert the soldiers before we were ready, and a line of *akicita* warriors did what they could to maintain discipline. As the sky began to pale we heard a soft owl-hoot, and another war party moved up alongside us; I saw it was Crazy Horse and his Oglalas, and for a moment I wished I were with them. Then I told myself it didn't make any difference; we were all fighting the same enemy, and who was with whom mattered much less than who did what. We had women and children and weak ones to protect, while the Bluecoats had no women except the paid ones who followed their camp, so our cause was the stronger. We were protecting our homes and families, while they were fighting for money.

In the gray morning light I saw Crazy Horse untie his long braids, which came below his waist, and shake out his hair the way a stallion shakes his mane. He put on his cape, which he'd made from the skin of a calf he shot out of the soldiers' herd earlier that year. It was red with white spots, and matched the cape he'd seen in his vision. Even in the semi-darkness, I could see the lightning slash on his cheek. Then he threw dust over the feet of his dappled war horse, and he was ready. Nearby, I saw Jack Red Cloud unroll a warbonnet and put it on, and I also saw the look of disgust on the older warriors' faces. Jack should have known that you earn the right to wear a warbonnet by being good in battle and not by having a famous father, but if he knew it he didn't pay any attention. With his silver rifle and his flowing headdress he looked all ready for war, but the others stood apart and would have nothing to do with him.

There was some firing as our scouts met with the Crow scouts from the soldiers, and then we moved forward and saw the soldiers in the valley. There were so many they seemed to fill the entire valley, and looked like a large herd of buffalo. Crazy Horse held back, but Little Hawk and our group moved forward, and then things began to happen. People who write about battles always make them look simple, saying these troops charged forward and these others retreated, and so the battle was won or lost, but when you're actually in one there is nothing but confusion. You see only what is in front of you at the moment, and you have no idea what is happening on the other parts of the field. I saw first a group of Crows charging at us, then something frightened them and they turned away, and through the dust and smoke I could see the Bluecoats. Some of them were mounted and some were afoot, and they were charging forward in short dashes, then lying down to fire. Crazy Horse and his warriors pulled back when the Bluecoats charged, and then all charged forward at once, shouting "Hoka hey!" and the soldiers broke and scattered. This was his plan, to work together instead of as individuals, and it seemed to work well.

The Cheyennes with whom I was fighting did it the old way, with warriors riding forward to count coup and show their bravery, and, while this suited me better, it was hard to be outstanding in all that confusion. I saw a lone trooper through the smoke and dust and charged at him with my lance, and just as he turned to face me there was a *thwik* and an arrow went into his open mouth, and out through the back of his neck. The look of surprise on his face was comical, and then blood poured out of his mouth and he began to topple off his horse, still clutching the reins. I counted coup on his back with my lance, and turned away.

Off to one side, I saw Chief Comes-in-Sight riding out

alone at the soldiers, waving his rifle and taunting them, and the bullets were kicking up puffs of dirt all around him. Then suddenly his horse reared and fell, and Comes-in-Sight sprang clear, took off the bridle to show he was unafraid, and began to dodge the bullets on foot. He seemed to be dancing in a cloud of dust. Here was a chance to show my courage; if I could save Comes-in-Sight from a spot like this, I'd be the hero of the battle. I urged my pony forward, lashing him with the rawhide quirt on my wrist, and, as I watched, another pony came out of the ranks, racing toward where Comes-in-Sight was zigzagging back and forth. It was Buffalo-Calf-Road-Woman, his sister, and she reached him, turned and presented her pony's rump to him, and he sprang up and they rode off together. Those of us who saw it set up a great shout and chanting, and even I, though disappointed, had to admire her. To the Cheyennes, the battle was thereafter known as The-Fight-Where-the-Girl-Saved-Her-Brother. (If you want to say it, it goes: "Kaē ē' sē wō ĭs tăn' ī wē ĭ tăt' ăn ē.") Other people called it the Battle of the Rosebud.

The main thing I remember, aside from the various flashes of action, was the screaming noise of the eagle-bone whistles. It cut through the gunfire and shouts and cries and the swishing of arrows, and it made a thin, high background to everything that happened. I heard much later that soldiers who'd been in that fight used to wake up nights with the noise of the whistles in their ears, so I guess it had its effect on both sides.

166

There were other things that happened, too, not all of them showing bravery. Young Jack Red Cloud had his pony killed under him, and instead of stopping to remove the bridle—a gesture that was universal among brave men— he started running at once, his silver-inlaid rifle clutched tightly in one hand and his warbonnet streaming out behind him. It was a disgusting sight, and three mounted Crows overtook him and began lashing him with their quirts, laughing at how easy it was to make him cry. They snatched the bonnet from his head and the rifle from his hands, and told him he was a little boy and ought not to be playing at being a warrior. This miserable spectacle was cut short when some Lakotas rode up and drove the Crows off, and brought the sobbing youth back to safety. I heard he never showed his face again, and went straight back to the agency. What he told his father about the rifle, no one knows.

In every battle there are odd things that happen, things you wouldn't believe, and I guess the oddest thing that day occurred when I had pulled back from the fighting, to let my pony rest. He was so tired I could scarcely whip him out of a walk, and I knew if I didn't let him breathe for a while he'd collapse. (I noticed Crazy Horse had the same problem; his dappled pony played out, and he had to change to a bay.) I was looking at the valley, trying to make some sense out of all the rushing back and forth, and all I could tell was that there seemed to be three separate fights on the same field, all broken up into charges and counter-charges. I was wondering how you could possibly tell who won such a fight,

167

when I caught the unmistakable smell of meat cooking. I could see nothing, but the smell was strong, so I led my pony to a nearby ridge and peered over. There, in a gully through which ran a creek, were four Lakotas who had killed and butchered a buffalo, and were roasting the meat! They waved and invited me to join them, and I must say I was tempted, because I'd had nothing to eat all day except a little *wasna* before sunrise. It seemed to me it would do no harm to have just a small piece, and it would give my pony more resting time. I had started down the gulley, my mouth watering in anticipation, when a big Lakota rode over the ridge. His face was smeared with dirt and grime over his war paint, and when he saw the four men eating he began to berate them. I stopped in my tracks as he reminded them of the helpless ones at home and the need for every man on the field, and in a shamefaced way they put down their meat, scattered the fire and trod out the embers, and mounted their ponies. They were still chewing as they filed past the angry chief. I was glad I hadn't been with them.

The battle lasted almost the entire day. Crazy Horse's tactics seemed to work well, because each time the Lakotas made a mass charge they broke up the soldiers, and kept them from forming into one big battle line the way they usually did. Still, it would have been hard to tell the winner if the Bluecoats hadn't started to withdraw. In the late afternoon, when the sun was settling toward the hills, the bugles set up a snarling chorus, and the soldiers began to pull back. Now they formed into one front, but it was a defensive front, and after a few more skirmishes the action was broken off. The field was littered with dead and wounded horses, soldiers, and Indians, and the noises made your stomach squirm. We gathered up our own and made travois for the more severely wounded, and we were astonished to find out that, after a full day of hard fighting, we had lost only eleven killed and five badly enough wounded to need help. Our scouts told us later that the soldiers had lost fifty-seven killed and wounded, including many of their Crow and Snake scouts, so on this basis we were the winners. Also, the soldiers were almost out of ammunition and had to go back to Goose Creek and wait for reinforcements and supplies, so we accomplished our aim of protecting our camp. Their aim had been to attack us and wipe us out, and in that they failed. It was the first time we'd come out on top in a pitched battle with the soldiers, and to a great extent it was because of Crazy Horse's tactics. Three Stars Crook, who'd been in charge of the soldiers, had some new thoughts about fighting Indians.

When you say we had "only" eleven killed that sounds very good, unless one of your family happens to be among the eleven. As we were slowly leaving the field, after having picked up every rifle, cartridge, and saddle bag we could find, I saw Lone Wolf leading his pony, and behind him another pony with a travois, and on the travois was a long bundle wrapped in a blanket. One moccasined foot stuck out of the blanket, and I remember how absolutely still it was, as though it was a part of the travois pole. I went alongside Lone Wolf, and saw his face: he was staring straight ahead, and his eyes were red and half closed. His war paint was smeared, his face was streaked and dirty, and the muscles along the side of his jaw twitched. For a while neither of us spoke, and then I said, "How did he get here?"

"He must have followed us." Lone Wolf's eyes remained half closed, unseeing.

"What happened?"

"I don't know. I didn't see him until they had him surrounded."

There was nothing I could say. The "only the earth and the sky last forever" line didn't seem particularly helpful at the moment, so I walked along in silence. The sky turned pink and then the light began to fade, and our whole war party straggled wearily back toward camp. There was some exultation, because we knew we'd done well, but a full day of fighting brought on such exhaustion that we had strength only to keep on moving. The time for celebration would come later, when we'd had some food and sleep. And in Lone Wolf's case, there would be no celebration. He had to present his father and mother with the body of their younger son. He didn't speak again until it was dark, and we were using the stars to guide us.

"I'm going to join the suicide boys," he said.

"Why do that?" The suicide boys were those who vowed to die fighting in the next battle, and nobody who took that vow ever survived. They were feasted and praised and made much of before the battle, and in some cases they inspired the other warriors to greater deeds, but the end result was always the same—the burial scaffold or burial tepee, and that was that. For someone Lone Wolf's age, it seemed pointless. "Isn't one death in your family enough?" I asked.

"I should have protected him. I didn't."

"It wasn't your fault."

"I failed. I have nothing more to live for."

There was no use talking to him, so I was silent. I thought of all the ceremonies that go on with the suicide boys, the songs and the feasting and the dancing, and I wondered how Lashuka would feel if I were to volunteer. *Then* her grandmother couldn't say I was a no-good; with everyone singing my praises and admiring my bravery, the old lady would have to break down and admit there was more to me than she'd thought. It would be a sweet revenge, to watch the expression on her face as the other suicide boys and I marched four times around the camp circle, with the medicine men and the Big Bellies and everyone saying how wonderful we were, and the women making their trilling noise for us; it would make her take back all her slurs and her scorn, and say I was the right person for Lashuka after all. Why not do it? Just to spite the old wolf-bitch, take the suicide vow and watch her grovel. Then I could have Lashuka. . . . For what? One night? I'd already had that, and more. Maybe not even one night, and then be killed. Coming down out of my dreams, I told myself there must be a better way than that. A suicide boy makes a very poor bridegroom.

Beside me, Lone Wolf walked along in silence, and the only sounds were the quiet thudding of many ponies' hooves, and the scraping of the travois poles across the earth.

10

Even before we returned from the battle, the various camps had started to move. It was always a good idea to move after a fight, in case the soldiers should come back with reinforcements, and while we weren't worried about Three Stars Crook at the moment there was the problem of food and game. An encampment as large as ours used up a great deal of grass for the ponies—there were perhaps twelve thousand of us, and I have no idea how many thousands of ponies

—and we had to be constantly on the move. Sitting Bull knew that up in the valley of the Greasy Grass, or Little Bighorn, there was good grazing land, and the scouts had reported many buffalo in the area, so we all went where Sitting Bull suggested, staying together for protection and always moving away from the soldiers.

There were some who thought his vision had already been fulfilled at the Rosebud, but, if you were to be precise about it, those soldiers hadn't exactly fallen into our camp; we had to go out and meet them, to keep them away. Also, there hadn't been so many killed; his vision had been of *many* soldiers, which meant there must be still something coming. Our scouts kept reporting Bluecoats in the area, but by now there was nothing new in that. They were everywhere.

Our new camp, once it was set up, was a great sight. The Greasy Grass flows in a northwesterly direction, squirming and wandering like a snake, and to the northeast a ridge of hills climbs away from the valley. As usual the Hunkpapa camp was farthest upstream and the Cheyenne farthest down, near where Medicine Tail creek flows into the Greasy Grass. Between the Hunkpapas and the Cheyennes were the Blackfoot Lakotas, the Minneconjoux, the Arrows-All-Gone, and the Oglalas, some along the banks of the river and some on the flat area leading to the benchland hills to the southwest, and here and there throughout the valley were scattered secondary camps of the many Indians who had come from all over to join us. When you looked on the valley from the surrounding hills you could see nothing but miles of tepees, with smoke rising from them, and along the outer edges the massive herds of grazing ponies. It made you feel good, just to look at it.

There was a lot of dancing and celebrating during the next few days, with everyone telling and retelling the various deeds that had been done. Of course the most spectacular deed was that of Buffalo-Calf-Road-Woman, and in her honor a four-day dance was held, at the end of which the sacred Buffalo Hat was brought out, decorated with a fresh scalp, and renewed. I should explain that the Cheyennes have two very sacred totems: the Four Arrows, which have been passed down from olden times and whose power is for men only, and the Buffalo Hat, which is chiefly for women but can benefit everybody. The Arrows are stone-tipped and very finely made, and are kept wrapped in fur taken from the back of a coyote, and bound in sinew. They are kept in the lodge of a holy man, whose job it is to care for them as long as he lives, and every now and then they are brought out and renewed, when someone wants to make a special cere-mony or prayer. The Hat is made from the skin of a buffalo cow, with elaborately painted horns attached to it, and it also is kept in the lodge of a special guardian. Both the Hat and the Arrows are powerful medicine; people pray to them and make sacrifices to them, and they heal the sick as well as bring good luck in war. Without them, the Cheyennes would be lost. Once long ago the Pawnees stole the Arrows, and the Cheyennes had nothing but bad luck until they got them back.

The scalp that was attached to the Hat was one taken from a Crow scout; the Cheyennes didn't consider white

174

men's scalps worth keeping. They would scalp a white man just for the sake of scalping him (there are those who claim that scalping was a white man's invention in the first place, when they put a bounty on the Indians they killed), but after the battle they would throw it away. They once scalped a white man's beard, but that was different. And I've already indicated that the white men scalped our women. Once you've seen that, you really don't care what you do to them.

Of all the ceremonies that took place that week, the most important for me was my induction into the Elk *akicita*. I couldn't believe it when Little Hawk came and asked me to join; I didn't think I'd done anything unusual in the battle, and I was almost resigned to the fact that I'd never become a great warrior. But he had apparently been watching me, and liked the way I held myself, and since the Elks had lost one man they needed a new member. I had a hard time hiding my joy, but I managed to look as though I was thinking it over before I accepted. Suddenly, everything began to look good. I tried to find Lashuka to tell her, but everywhere I looked she had just gone someplace else, so after looking all the places I could think of I gave up, and decided to save it.

Aside from the dances and the ceremonies, a lot of work was done. The hunters went out after buffalo and antelope, the women cooked the meat and tanned the hides, and Crazy Horse took a group of boys back to the battlefield to scavenge around and pick up anything usable that was left. They came back with several sacks full of shell cases, ammunition belts, horseshoes, arrows, lance tips—anything that could be re-used, and fashioned into a weapon. They even picked up spent and misshapen bullets, to be hammered back into form, and retrieved many rifles that had jammed and been broken or thrown away. (The soldiers had a lot of trouble with their repeating rifles, which jammed when they got too hot, so one Indian trick was to rush at them and make them fire fast three times, after which many of the rifles quit. We had people who could unjam them when they cooled.)

One day, about a week after the battle, the Elks had guard duty in the Cheyenne camp, and I was assigned to watch the lodge of the keeper of the Buffalo Hat. It was a warm, sunny day, the smells of the grass and the flowers mingled with the comforting smells of the camp, and it was hard to believe there was trouble anywhere. There was some talk of having games and wrestling matches and races between the *akicitas,* but there was a lot of work to be done, and several families were still in mourning, so it was thought best to wait awhile. I hadn't seen Lone Wolf since the night after the battle, although I'd seen his parents in the distance— his mother with her clothes and arms slashed, and his father with his hair cut short. I wondered if they knew of Lone Wolf's plans, and my heart grew tight for them.

When the sun was almost overhead I saw Laughing Hawk approaching from the Oglala camp, and I greeted him. He acknowledged the greeting in an offhand way, and came and sat next to me. His hair was wet, and his skin glistened.

"Have you been swimming?" I asked. The idea sounded appealing, and I wished my guard duty were over.

He nodded. "We had a scalp dance last night," he said. "The sun was coming up when I went to sleep. I just got up."

"We had four days of dancing," I said.

"I heard about that."

"We've named the battle in her honor."

"I heard that, too. I don't know what we're going to call it." He picked a sprig of grass, and put it in his mouth. "I heard a strange thing," he said. "After my swim I got some food from an old lady, and she told me the soldiers were coming today."

"How does she know that?"

He took the grass from his mouth, and examined it. "She wouldn't say. She just said she knew."

"I don't believe her. The scouts say Three Stars is going the other way."

"Well, you know how old ladies are." He nibbled at the root end of the grass. "They're always having visions."

We saw Crazy Horse go past, apparently having come to the Cheyenne camp for a visit. He seemed withdrawn into himself, which he often was, and he didn't notice me. I wanted to tell him about my joining the Elks, but I didn't want to be the one to speak first. When Crazy Horse was in one of his moods, you left him alone. Then I saw Lashuka, heading upstream along the river bank, and I wondered what errand her grandmother was sending her on now. If I hadn't had the guard duty I would have gone to speak to her, but I couldn't leave the medicine lodge until I'd been relieved.

177

Those were the rules, and you can be sure I wasn't going to break them. So I watched her go, until she was out of sight. If I'd known then how the day was going to end, I would have broken all the rules. Or called to her, or something. I guess it's probably just as well I didn't know. There are some things that shouldn't be learned in advance.

Laughing Hawk saw my eyes as they followed her, and he said, "Is that your girl?"

"Yes," I said.

"I can't tell from here. Is she pretty?"

"Yes."

"Why don't you marry her?"

"Her grandmother wants forty horses."

"That's a lot. Who has forty horses?"

"I think if I could make a name for myself, she might ask less. She'd rather have a famous warrior in the family than anything else."

"Then it's simple. Become a famous warrior."

I looked at him, and smiled. "What do you think I've been trying to do?"

He laughed. "I guess a lot depends on luck. Or how good your medicine is. Did you see Crazy Horse in that last battle?"

"A few times."

"That man has strong medicine. He'd lead a charge until the soldiers broke, then he'd jump off his pony to shoot. He never shot once from horseback, and he never missed what he shot at. And he wasn't touched. That is strong medicine."

"How did you do?"

"I survived. I shot at a few soldiers, but I don't know if I hit any. I suppose I must have. But with that new way of fighting, you can't be sure. You all act together, and don't go after coups and scalps."

"It seems to work."

There was a commotion off to the south, and some shouting, and we looked toward the Oglala camp circle and could see people running about. Some were running toward the pony herd; women were hurriedly rounding up their children, and in the far distance a cloud of dust hung above the hills. Then a wild-eyed Oglala came galloping toward our camp, shouting: "Soldiers coming here! Many white men are attacking!"

Laughing Hawk jumped up and raced away for his pony, and I translated the alarm into Cheyenne for the benefit of our camp. At the same moment distant shots could be heard, and people began to run this way and that. The women's first instinct was to find their children, and then to start packing to make ready in case we had to flee camp. The warriors began to oil, paint, and dress themselves for battle, and the older men and the Big Bellies circulated through the camp, calming those who were afraid and doing what they could to lessen the confusion. They were the guardians of the weak and helpless while the warriors were away, and their presence was very soothing.

I, gnawing my knuckles in frustration, had to stay by the medicine tent until I was relieved, and I had to watch from the side as Two Moon got together a war party. Boys had run out and brought in the ponies, and in a short while the group was painted, armed, and mounted, and the ponies danced and skittered about, raising clouds of dust. The warriors shouted "Hay-ay! Hay-ay!" the Cheyenne war chant, waiting for Two Moon to lead them off. The firing in the distance was heavier, and it sounded closer.

Two Moon raised his Remington over his head, and in a loud, almost piercing voice called out: "Warriors! Warriors! Don't run away if the soldiers charge you! Stand and fight! Watch me! I shall fight until I am killed!" They responded with a roar of "Hay-ay! Hay-ay!" and then in almost an instant they were gone, leaving only the cloud of dust behind them. The drumming of their ponies' hooves mingled with the sounds of firing, and the distant shouts.

Finally I was relieved, by an Elk who'd been wounded at the Rosebud and was not yet fit for battle, and I rushed to my tepee to paint and arm myself. I was in such a hurry that I didn't do a very good job; I just smeared the paint on quickly, grabbed my rifle, ammunition, bow and arrows, and lance, and went for my pony. I was determined to catch up with Two Moon's war party, wherever they had gone. I had no fear now; the only thing I was afraid of was that I might be too late.

When I had mounted my pony and was ready to start, I saw three Cheyennes looking at something across the river, where Medicine Tail creek joins the Greasy Grass. One of them, Slow Bear, was pointing, and I looked where he pointed and was astonished to see mounted troopers coming down the coulee.

180

"We must stop them!" Slow Bear shouted. "Come on!"

The four of us rode toward the river, and I must say I was wondering how we were going to stop a whole troop of soldiers. I wasn't made any more confident by an old man named Mad Wolf, who rode alongside us on a rickety horse and tried to make us turn back. "Wait until our brothers come to help!" he kept pleading. "Don't throw your lives away like this!"

Finally, Slow Bear lost patience. "Uncle, only the earth and the sky last long," he said. "If the four of us can save the camp, our lives will go to a good cause."

That stopped Mad Wolf, and he turned away, still whining.

We dismounted behind a ridge this side of the river, and then saw that the soldiers were chasing five Lakotas, who were riding at full speed down the coulee to the river. There was a ford at that place, and as the Lakotas splashed across we fired at the soldiers and also at their Crow scouts, who were on a bluff overlooking the river. We hit a few soldiers as they tried to cross the ford, and one of them, a man in a buckskin shirt, fell into the water and was dragged out by his companions. The five Lakotas joined us, although they had no rifles, and a Cheyenne named White Shield also came in, so we had ten men to defend the ford. This was a good deal better than four, and I felt more confident.

After that first time, the soldiers didn't try to cross the river again. They fell back and kept shooting at us from a distance, and we returned the fire, ducking behind rocks and changing places to look like more than we were. It was a

181

pointless sort of fight, except that we were defending the camp. All we had to do was keep them from crossing the river, and after the man in the buckskin shirt was hit they seemed content to stay on the other side.

How long this went on I don't remember; the sun was high and the air was hot and full of dust and powder smoke, and the action was just a succession of duck, run, and fire, duck, run, and fire, and so on. I tried to make every shot count, but I have no idea if I hit anyone or not. My mouth was dry and tasted of dirt, and I wished I could go to the river for a drink.

Then from behind us came the drumming of many hooves and a roar of "Hoka hey!" and Crazy Horse and the Oglalas came charging up. His hair was loose and streaming out behind him, his two feathers fluttering in the wind. He wore his spotted red calfskin cape, and his shoulders were painted red, and with the lightning streaks on his cheeks he looked like some sort of raging demon. They rode down the stream a way and then crossed over, to get on the other side of the soldiers. Next came Two Moon and his Cheyennes, and I decided they must have finished the first fight, and be coming back to help in this one. The soldiers across the river fell back even farther, and I joined Two Moon and the others as we hurried to follow them.

From there on, the battle became a succession of flashes of memory, like the Rosebud fight. The soldiers were gathered at the top of a rise, while we came at them from all sides, some making mass charges with Crazy Horse, and

182

others creeping through the sagebrush and snapping off shots when the dust cleared enough to see anything. I was told later, by a woman who watched from a distance, that the top of the rise was one big cloud of dust and smoke, out of which riderless horses would come running. She said it was impossible to tell what was happening, any more than you could tell from the middle of the action.

The hand-to-hand fighting was started by the suicide boys. Lakota runners came along the ridge where we were firing, and they called out to watch for the suicide boys and be ready to jump up and follow them once they went in. I translated this into Cheyenne, and we all waited for them to appear. Finally I saw them, four Lakotas and my friend Lone Wolf, and they rode up from the river, stampeding some of the troopers' gray horses on the way, and then they galloped right into the midst of the troopers, and we came in from all sides behind them. From there on, it was just one big, wild scramble. Not one of the suicide boys survived—Lone Wolf died of his wounds during the night—but they started the fighting that brought the battle to an end. I remember thinking, as I watched Lone Wolf ride into the Bluecoats and disappear like a stone in a lake, that there went the boy who, a short while ago, had been thinking of going back to the agency, and letting the white men take care of him. Well, I thought, the white men took care of him all right, and it was a stupid waste of a young man's life.

I remember seeing White Bull, Sitting Bull's nephew, wearing a long-tailed warbonnet and fighting with a trooper who had him by the hair and was trying to bite off his nose. Two Lakotas clubbed the trooper to the ground, and White Bull beat him to death with his rifle. I remember the clouds of arrows that some of the Indians shot in the air, the metal tips twinkling in the sun as they hung and then started down, and then the screaming of the horses as the arrows landed among them. I remember seeing Gall, the Hunkpapa war chief, beating a trooper's brains out with his hatchet, and continuing to pound the shattered skull long after life had gone. (I later found out that all of Gall's family had been rubbed out in that first charge, which had been made by Major Reno's men on the Hunkpapa camp.) I remember seeing a trooper rush off on his horse with one Lakota and two Cheyennes after him, and when he reached the end of the gully he stopped, drew his pistol, and shot himself in the head. A Cheyenne youth named Big Beaver, who'd been watching the fight from a hillside, galloped to where the trooper lay, took his pistol and cartridge belt, and galloped back up the hill again. And I remember seeing a Lakota warrior walking slowly away from the fight, with his whole lower jaw shot off. A lot of things happened that day, and everybody has his own memories.

Finally the pace of the fighting died down, and the only soldiers left were a group on the west end of the ridge, who had hidden behind their dead horses. They fired only as they saw an Indian, and the Indians showed themselves only to jump up from behind a sagebrush, fire, and then flatten out again. From where I was, I could see the whole

184

north slope of the ridge was thick with hidden Indians, creeping slowly closer to the barricade of dead horses. There must have been a thousand or more; I couldn't count their numbers, but they were behind every bush and stone, and the hill was crawling with them. The soldiers couldn't see them; the only Indians they could see were those who jumped up to fire, and the only other thing they could see were the arrows that kept raining down among them. The only protection from those arrows was to crawl under their horses, and of course from there they couldn't shoot.

There was a rush of Indians to the crest of the ridge, and then silence. Everywhere you looked there were dead soldiers and their horses, with arrows bristling from them like tufts of buffalo grass. Someone later made a count, and said there were two hundred and sixty-one soldiers, against I don't know how many thousand of us. We lost anywhere from thirty-five to sixty-five dead, depending on whom you listen to. Each group took care of its own dead, so it was hard to come to a final count.

Then the women and children came scrambling up the slope, stripping the bodies, taking what they wanted from them, and in some cases cutting them up pretty badly. There was a lot of green paper lying around, and also round bits of white metal, which was apparently the soldiers' pay money, and some people took the white metal to hammer into buckles, while others made playthings for the children out of the green paper. Some few, who knew what the money meant, collected it in bags and hid it, although now nobody can remember where. What most people wanted were the soldiers' jackets, and, of course, their guns and ammunition. There wasn't much ammunition left, but there were plenty of pistols and rifles.

There is a sort of letdown when a battle is over, and you walk around in a daze wondering what to do next. Sometimes you laugh at things that aren't really very funny, like the woman who had stripped a soldier naked and was about to cut off his manhood when he jumped up, having only been pretending to be dead. He started fighting with the woman, and two other women joined in and stabbed him, and pretty soon he really was dead. We laughed a lot about that, although it wasn't very funny for him. Things like that, after a battle, get more laughter than they deserve.

I saw another soldier who had been stripped—in the end, not one of them was left with any clothing—and he had two small bullet holes in his chest. An old woman and a younger one were looking at him, and the old woman leaned down and took her bone sewing awl and drove it first into one of his ears, and then into the other. Straightening up, she said, "Now Long Hair will hear better in the Spirit Land." It never occurred to me that it might have been Custer because his hair was cut short, but it was the color yellow that had been described, so I guess it really was he. This was confirmed later, which made a lot of people feel good.

I've been going into all this detail about the battle because I don't want to tell what happened next, but now I guess I have to. Word came up the hill that some of Major Reno's men, who'd made the first attack and been beaten off, were hiding in the trees across the river from the Hunkpapa camp, and we were going to try to flush them out. I went down to the ford and toward the camps, and I could see people making travois for the dead and wounded, and hear the keening of the wives and mothers whose men had been killed. It was a sad time for many, but I didn't feel either good or bad; I was happy we'd rubbed the soldiers out, but I wondered what was going to happen next, and how many more times we'd have to do it before they let us alone. Something told me they wouldn't ever let us alone; that they'd keep coming back in larger and larger numbers, until we were the ones who were rubbed out. This took some of the pleasure out of the victory, and I could only hope I was wrong.

I heard a keening as I approached the Hunkpapa camp, and I saw the silent, blanket-wrapped figures of Gall's wife and children, and his bullet-shredded lodge. Reno's soldiers must have come very close in their first charge, in order to do that much damage. There were other blanket-wrapped figures, too, and my throat closed when I saw that Lashuka's grandmother was one of the mourners. Another old woman was with her, holding her by her arms, and their clothing was in disarray, their hair tangled with dirt, and their arms slashed. The other woman looked at me as I approached, and continued her keening.

"Who is it?" I asked, not wanting to know.

Neither of them spoke, and I kneeled down and pulled

187

the blanket aside, and saw her face. She looked peaceful, as though sleeping, and she was as beautiful as I ever saw her, but her skin was cold as a snake's. I put the blanket back, gently, looked toward the hill where Reno's men were, and started for the river.

I think I would probably have charged the hill alone, but there were others there who stopped me. They told me we had the soldiers trapped; we were picking them off as their thirst drove them to the river for water, and I wouldn't get halfway up the hill before they shot me. They were well dug in, and our best plan was to wait. So I settled down, to kill as many of them as I could.

Which wasn't many. Three hours after the battle the first lodges were taken down and the people began to move, some to the agency and some farther north, into the hills and across the border to the country now known as Canada. Next day, when we were thinking of a charge up the hill, word came that reinforcements were on the way for the Bluecoats, and we'd best move out. We didn't have the means to fight another big battle that soon. So we left.

I tried to find Lashuka's grandmother, but she must have gone among the earlier ones, and I didn't know where. I couldn't imagine her going back to the agency, but I also couldn't think of anything else. I looked among the burial tepees and the scaffolds, and finally, on a scaffold far away from the camp, I saw a blanket I recognized. I stood beneath the rickety scaffold, trying to talk to the blanket. I tried to imagine that Lashuka was at her forest lake in the *Paha Sapa*, the one she saw when she dreamed of the future, but it was no good. It didn't work, because all I was doing was talking to a wrinkled red blanket, and finally I turned away and went to the Oglala camp. The Cheyennes had nothing more for me, and with the Oglalas there was at least Crazy Horse, and freedom.

If you could count that for anything; in little more than a year he was bayoneted to death by a reservation Bluecoat, while Little Big Man held his arms. After that I stopped trying for freedom, because it didn't seem to mean much. It means whatever the winner wants it to mean, and nothing more.

BIBLIOGRAPHY

Berger, Thomas, *Little Big Man,* New York: Dial Press, 1964

Brown, Dee, *Bury My Heart at Wounded Knee,* New York: Holt, Rinehart & Winston, 1970. *Showdown at Little Bighorn,* New York: Berkley Publishing Corp., 1964

Grinnell, George Bird, *The Fighting Cheyennes,* Norman: University of Oklahoma Press, 1956

Hassrick, Royal B., *The Sioux,* Norman: University of Oklahoma Press, 1964

Hyde, George E., *Red Cloud's Folk,* Norman: University of Oklahoma Press, 1936

Lampman, Evelyn Sibley, *Once Upon the Little Bighorn,* New York: Thomas Y. Crowell, 1971

Marquis, Thomas B., *Wooden Leg,* Minneapolis: Bison Books from the Midwest Co., 1931

Miller, David Humphreys, *Echoes of the Little Bighorn,* New York: American Heritage, Vol. XXII, No. 4, June 1971

Neihardt, John G., *Black Elk Speaks,* Lincoln: Bison Books from University of Nebraska Press, 1961

Sandoz, Mari, *Crazy Horse,* New York: Bison Books from Hastings House, 1942

Stands in Timber, John (with Margot Liberty and Robert M. Utley), *Cheyenne Memories,* New Haven: Yale University Press, 1967

Other great books from
HARPER TROPHY

■ HarperCollins*Publishers*

10 East 53rd Street, New York, NY 10022.